JFIC
Howell

W9-CCJ-228

HIGH SCORE

Destiny Howell

SCHOLASTIC PRESS
NEW YORK

Copyright © 2022 by Destiny Howell

All rights reserved. Published by Scholastic Press, an imprint of Scholastic Inc., *Publishers since 1920*. SCHOLASTIC, SCHOLASTIC PRESS, and associated logos are trademarks and/or registered trademarks of Scholastic Inc.

The publisher does not have any control over and does not assume any responsibility for author or third-party websites or their content.

No part of this publication may be reproduced, stored in a retrieval system, or transmitted in any form or by any means, electronic, mechanical, photocopying, recording, or otherwise, without written permission of the publisher. For information regarding permission, write to Scholastic Inc., Attention: Permissions Department, 557 Broadway, New York, NY 10012.

This book is a work of fiction. Names, characters, places, and incidents are either the product of the author's imagination or are used fictitiously, and any resemblance to actual persons, living or dead, business establishments, events, or locales is entirely coincidental.

Library of Congress Cataloging-in-Publication Data available

ISBN 978-1-338-74671-6

10 9 8 7 6 5 4 3 2 1   22 23 24 25 26

Printed in Italy   183

First edition, June 2022

Book design by Yaffa Jaskoll and Stephanie Yang

TO MY MOM AND DAD, FOR ENDURING COUNTLESS
SUNDAYS SURROUNDED BY SCREAMING CHILDREN
AND PINGING ARCADE CABINETS SO MY BROTHER
AND I COULD STOMP ON CARTOON SPIDERS

Chapter One
A FISTFUL OF TICKETS

Group project day had arrived, which meant that I was suddenly the most popular kid in class. When it comes time for gym, I'm radioactive—but the second Mr. Conover announced we were doing group presentations on natural disasters, I felt about twenty pairs of eyeballs shift toward me.

I might have started at Ella Fitzgerald Middle School a year later than most kids, but my rep spread pretty quickly: If you want an A on a class project, make sure DJ's in your group. I didn't do anything to advertise it, but I didn't try to stop it either. There are worse things to be known for.

"Not yet," Mr. Conover said as kids started to move from their seats. "I don't want everyone to just partner up with their friends. I've already assigned teams." He ignored the low moan that rolled through the class like thunder. "Once you hear your teammates, you can go find them and use the last few minutes of class to plan." He called off two sets of four names before I heard mine.

"Group 3: Volcanic Eruptions. DJ. Maria. Tyler. Topher."

As I heard the names, my brain automatically started spitting out possibilities for our project. I knew Maria was a fantastic baker. She'd probably love making a volcano model out of cake. And the class would love the chance to get to eat cake in class. Topher was convinced that he was Weird Al's long-lost son. He'd love a chance to rewrite "Under Pressure" to make it about volcanoes and perform it in front of the class. And Tyler could—

I shook my head as I got up to join my group. Simple. Keep it simple. People like simple.

When I got to the corner of the room where my group was, Tyler slapped me on the back, which just felt weird. Tyler's the kind of guy girls whisper about all giggly when they're in their little groups—but he looks like a seventh-grade version of Clark Kent, so I can't really blame them. Meanwhile, I dressed up as James Bond for Halloween one year and almost every single house I went to thought I was a businessman. I mean, I'm Black, so I'm never gonna be a dead ringer for Daniel Craig, but I was carrying a martini glass! How many businessmen go to work, cocktail in hand?

Anyway, my point is our coolness levels are nowhere near the same, but here I was, getting a backslap like we were buddies.

"Deej," he said, giving my nickname a nickname, because he was just that cool. "My man. So, what are we doing? What's the plan?"

My complicated ideas spontaneously bubbled back to the top of my brain. Maybe instead of a big volcano cake, we could do mini-molten lava cakes with the chocolate dyed orange-red like actual lava. And we could do a whole music video and film it before the presentation. I could ask the AV Club to borrow some video equipment and—

"Deej?" Tyler said, snapping me back to reality.

"What? Oh, right." I did my best to rein in my brain. "Right, OK. I'll do the research. Tyler, you can type the important parts into a PowerPoint. Maria, you can find the pictures. Topher, you can do most of the talking. It should be an easy A for everyone."

That was clearly what they wanted to hear. I had no arguments from anyone about the assignment split—probably because I'd given myself the bulk of the work. But it was the only way to make sure things got done properly.

We barely had time to exchange cell numbers before the bell rang. I slung my backpack over my shoulder and started toward my locker, when I felt someone tap me from behind. It was Tyler again.

"Hey, buddy," he said, giving me a friendly punch on the arm. "Listen, I have a big favor to ask. You know we have a big baseball game coming up, right? Against the Timberwolves."

There wasn't a single person at school who didn't know, what with the banners that were plastered all over the hallway walls. My old school had been a basketball school, but the Fitz was definitely a baseball school. And, adding to his list of selling points, Tyler was the star player of our team, the Rockets. He was like one of those products they have infomercials about: He catches! He pitches! He juliennes carrots! What *can't* he do?

"I'm gonna have to do a lot of practicing this week so, you know, I was wondering if—"

"You want me to do your part of the project," I finished for him.

He gave me a sheepish smile. "I usually wouldn't ask, but I really don't have the time, and I know you're good at these projects and—"

"It's fine," I said, before he wasted any more energy trying to convince me. "I don't mind."

"I don't want you to think I'm being lazy or anything," he said, like he didn't believe me. "I'd do it if we didn't have this big game, but—"

"Really, it's not a big deal," I said. I'd only split up the work so we could say to Mr. Conover that we all helped without lying. "I'm doing all the research anyway. I might as well type it into the PowerPoint too."

"That's just what I was thinking," he said with another backslap. Two backslaps from Tyler in one day. If people were paying attention, my social standing was going to get a boost. "Great minds, right?"

"Sure," I said. I was about to turn down the hallway to where my locker was, when Tyler stopped me.

"Hey, wait. Take this." He took my hand and pressed something into my palm. I knew what it was before I looked down: a brick of Starcade tickets.

"Tyler, I don't—" As I tried to give them back to him, he raised his hands up so I couldn't.

"You're the man, Deej," he said, giving me finger guns before melting into the rest of the crowd.

I sighed as I pushed the tickets into my pocket and headed toward my locker.

Every school has a currency: contraband candy, rubber bracelets, actual money if you go to a school full of rich kids. At my old school it was these holographic trading cards from Japan. At the Fitz, it's Starcade tickets, which makes sense since there's a Starcade literally across the street.

It's one of the favorite hangout spots for kids looking to relax after a long day at school. With the smell of pizza in the air and the sound of dozens of game machines pinging around you, it's hard to think about whatever bad thing happened in gym or how you probably failed that pop quiz in English. And, on top of that, most of the game machines spit out tickets that can be redeemed for pretty good prizes. Not just little things like candy or stickers. On the top shelves, there are cameras and game systems and other big-ticket items.

Pretty much any kid with the tiniest bit of self-control was saving for one of those top-shelf items, which meant that a handful of tickets to the right person could get you anything from a stick of gum to the locker combination of your least-favorite classmate.

It wasn't so much the kids looking to trade tickets for Twinkies that I wanted to avoid by taking tickets from

Tyler. Once it got out that you would do schoolwork for tickets, it was only a matter of time before that was your thing, and every lazy kid with an essay to write and some extra tickets lying around was hounding you at lunch, trying to hire you. Because of that, I tried to stay away from any even semi-shady ticket transactions.

But if it was just Tyler this once, it was probably OK. And if anyone brought it up, I could just say I made an exception for the golden boy. Everyone did.

When I opened my locker door, a green slip of paper fell out. I caught it before it hit the floor, and crunched it into a little ball. There was a new one in my locker every Monday like clockwork, and I always tossed them. So did a lot of kids. But a lot of kids didn't, which meant that Lucky's little lottery side hustle did good business.

You know how some people are rich because they're famous, and some people are famous because they're rich? Well, Lucas "Lucky" Ford was in that second category. Apparently, his older cousin had been some kind of

Skee-Ball genius. When his family moved cross-country to California where they don't have any Starcades, the cousin gave Lucky his stash of tickets. That alone probably would have been enough to put him in the top half of ticket holders at school, but Lucky wasn't just lucky. He was smart too. He didn't just spend tickets. He figured out ways to turn tickets into more tickets. One of those ways was the Lucky Lotto. For five tickets (attached to a green, official, Lucky Lotto entry slip and slipped into Lucky's locker before Friday), any kid could have a chance to win a five-hundred-ticket jackpot.

Of course, since there were about a thousand kids at the Fitz and around a third of them played the lotto on a regular basis, that meant Lucky was making double that five-hundred-ticket prize every week.

I didn't want anything to do with it, but I had to respect the hustle.

I swapped out my science textbook for my math textbook, slammed my locker door, and—

"Oof."

I immediately walked directly into the back of someone significantly taller than me. "Sorry, Mr.—" I started, but when the guy turned around, I realized it wasn't a teacher. It was a student. I didn't know him personally, but I'd seen him around. He was hard to miss, seeing as he was as tall as most of the teachers, broad as a linebacker, and he wore the same green military jacket all the time like a cartoon character.

He looked even bigger than usual now that I was face-to . . . well face-to-chest with him, looking up at his thick, frowning eyebrows and faint wisps of blond chin hair. I'd overheard bits of gossip about him over the past few months. That he was an exchange student from Russia. That he was expelled from his last school for fighting a teacher . . . and winning. That he'd been held back four times. That all three were true. I took the rumors with a grain of salt, but none of it seemed that far-fetched right now.

I took a quick step away from him. "Whoa. I meant . . ." Shoot, what was his name? I had no idea. I'd just been calling him "That One Scary Tall Dude" in my head. "Bro," I improvised. "Yeah. Sorry, bro."

He grunted at me and then lumbered away. I watched him go for a few seconds before sighing in relief, putting my book under my arm, and heading for class before I got myself into any more trouble.

Chapter Two
A FAMILIAR FACE

Math class went by more quickly than usual, mainly because Duke was home sick. I think every school has at least one Duke. The kind of kid who will do anything if he thinks it'll get him the tiniest bit of attention. One time, I heard Duke say that he would do anything on a dare for fifty tickets. And he said it like he was proud of himself.

I have two classes with him, homeroom and math, and every day he treats the entirety of both of them (at least until he gets kicked out) like he's auditioning for *SNL*. He makes sound effects when the teacher turns around, he answers questions doing terrible impressions, and he has this recurring bit where he pretends like Duke is his title instead of his name and tries to get people to call him

"Your Majesty." It's like one of those dumb, online prank channels, except I can't just unsubscribe from math class.

To be fair, some people think Duke is funny. To be even more fair, some people also think raisins belong in oatmeal cookies. People are wrong all the time.

When the bell rang, I made my way to the cafeteria. As I walked in, I stopped to take a look at the bulletin board. There was nothing new: flyers about the upcoming baseball game, notices about a PTA meeting that had happened a week ago, and a signup sheet for the school musical (*The Little Mermaid Jr.*) that I'd been trying to ignore for the past week.

I'd brought my lunch, so I skipped the line and made my way to my usual table, near the back. It was basically the designated loner table, which was fine. Loner means you're sitting alone because you want to. It wasn't the *loser* table. That one was two tables down—except no one called it that. They called it Pluto, which I know makes zero sense unless you go to the Fitz, so let me explain.

Remember how our team name is the Rockets? Well,

three years back, the principal started this thing called Rocket Boosters. The idea was that there would be a box in the front office where anyone could anonymously say something nice about another student, and then one of the student anchors would read some of them during the morning announcements.

This went about how you'd think. A couple of students used it the way it was intended, but people mainly just stuffed the box with jokes and stuff that the news kids couldn't possibly say over the intercom, so it kind of died away.

Until the year before I showed up.

It was midway through the year. Lucky was in sixth grade, and he'd already launched the cornerstones of his black market hustles: running junk food from the boys' bathroom, outsourcing homework from slackers to cash-strapped and morally flexible nerds, and, of course, the Lucky Lotto.

The lotto was his first hustle. His pet project. I mean, he named it after himself. It's how he made his rep.

Which is why it ticked him off so much when Bruno Zapinski tried to rig it.

Now, Bruno was bold, I'll give him that. But he wasn't very smart.

I don't know how Bruno did it, but he managed to break into Lucky's locker where he used to keep the entry slips and swapped out all of them for ones with Bruno's name. Which might have worked if Lucky didn't look at any other slip in the box, even by accident.

Tip for any of you out there planning on tangling with the kingpin of your school's underground: They probably didn't get that position by being sloppy.

So, Lucky noticed right away. Bruno never got his hands on the tickets. But Lucky couldn't let that stand. And he couldn't let Bruno off with a slap on the wrist either. I mean, if it seemed like any idiot could mess with him and get away with it, his reputation would go down the tubes.

A different person would have paid some eighth graders to beat Bruno up. Lucky definitely had the tickets for it.

But Lucky wanted to send a message. He wanted everyone to know that he wasn't just a kid who'd fallen into a small fortune in tickets. He was someone who shouldn't be messed with.

The next day, for the first time in months, there was a Rocket Booster announcement during the morning announcements.

"Shout-out to Bruno. I feel so *lucky* he goes to this school."

Then, between homeroom and first period, he somehow ended up with two black eyes.

I don't know if people put it together or if Lucky set up a whisper campaign to get the word out, but the news spread pretty quickly that Lucky had put his stamp of disapproval on Bruno, and that was the result. Anyone who didn't figure it out then did next week when Anita Dickens snitched to the principal about Lucky's junk food operation and, one Rocket Booster shout-out later, found herself on the business end of a water balloon full of toilet water. Or two weeks later, when Owen Geis tried starting his own lotto, which resulted in a Rocket Booster shout-out and a time-delayed backpack stink bomb that went off in the band room midway through "America the Beautiful."

After that, the physical force wasn't even necessary. The threat was enough. Lucky got you rocket boosted and, bam—you were blacklisted. People were so scared that Lucky's punishment might splash onto them if they associated with someone who'd gotten rocket boosted that they stopped hanging out with them. It was awful, but effective.

Which brings me back to Pluto. If you get into a rocket ship and blast off, Pluto is about as far away from civilization as you can get while still technically being in the solar system. Which is pretty much what your school life is like once you've been rocket boosted.

I pulled out my sandwich and took a bite as I scanned the cafeteria. It was the usual organized chaos. Jock dudes roughhousing at one table. Japan geeks swapping manga at another table. Softball girls . . . wait, was one missing?

Where was she? I started looking for her before squeezing my eyes shut.

None of your business, DJ, I told myself, taking another bite of my sandwich. *Leave it alone.*

When I opened my eyes again, I instead turned to the table directly to my right, which was full of kids on their phones in serious concentration while other kids leaned in, watching over their shoulders, cheering and booing.

The only person sitting at the table who wasn't on their phone was Mariposa Diaz. Four-foot-nothing Mariposa, with her long, dark hair, dusting of freckles, and an expression that looked like it belonged on an executioner. She was Lucky's right-hand girl. He'd hire just about anyone for simple things like delivering lotto flyers or roughing someone up, but if he really needed something done and he couldn't do it himself, he sent her. And, right now, she was running qualifiers for the Rexcellent tournament he had going.

It was one of Lucky's more recent innovations in separating people from their tickets. Rexcellent Racers was a mobile derby game that had gotten really popular in the past couple of months. You played as a racer in a tricked-out dino-themed derby car, and your goal was to win the race by smashing up the other racers' cars as much as possible. There was the Alloslammer. The Vicious Velociraptor. The T-Wrecks (obviously).

He set up a tournament, open to everyone in the school. Qualifying rounds, knockout eliminations, the whole nine yards. The entry fee was a hefty five hundred tickets, but the prize was fifty thousand tickets. Fifty thousand! That was enough to make anyone who thought they had even half a chance try their luck. Besides, I didn't think Lucky had set up the tournament to make money so much as to prove that he could give away fifty thousand tickets and still be the richest guy around. Any extra he made was a bonus.

Suddenly, about half the tournament table erupted in cheers. Clearly, they'd just qualified. Mariposa dutifully wrote down the names of the winners in a notebook before saying, "OK, next group. Let's go. We don't have all day."

The kids got up and were replaced with another set, phones in hand, determination in their eyes. They each handed Mariposa a blue slip of paper, which she scanned before nodding and letting them sit.

"Looks like a solid operation," I heard a voice say from the other side of the table. A very familiar voice. *But it couldn't be him*, I thought as I turned. I was at the Fitz now and he was back at—

"Conor?!"

It *was* him. Same shaggy brown hair. Same gangly limbs. Same chipped-tooth grin from the time he jumped off the jungle gym and ate pavement. Everything was the same, except he was sliding into the seat across from mine instead of across town at Grover Cleveland Middle School where he was supposed to be.

As I gaped at him, he just smiled wider. "Hey, DJ. What's up?"

Chapter Three
NEW KID ON THE BLOCK

"WHAT ARE YOU—?!" I yelled so loudly you could almost hear it over the background roar of the cafeteria, so I stopped and tried again. "What are you doing here?"

He snorted. "What, you're not happy to see your best friend? Ouch, dude."

The tips of my ears burned with guilt. He didn't seem actually annoyed with me, but I had low-key ghosted Conor all summer. I'd told myself that it was what was best for both of us, but all those one-word responses and declined invitations bubbled up in my mind like toxic waste.

"No, I'm just—I don't—how are you here?" I almost wanted to poke his face to make sure I wasn't having an elaborate hallucination, but as Conor shoved a handful of fries into his mouth and started talking with his mouth full, the little bits of fries that hit my face convinced me that this was really happening.

"School was lame without you, so I got transferred. Besides, I wasn't gonna let you go it alone here. Isn't it great?"

"How?"

"How is it great?"

"No! How did you get transferred?"

"*You* got transferred," he pointed out.

"Yeah, but not in the middle of the school year! And . . . you know. It was different." I shook off the memory. "Seriously, how did you get here? They don't just let you change schools for no reason."

"I had a reason," he said proudly. "I was being bullied."

Now I snorted. "No, you weren't." I'd practically been friends with Conor since we were both in diapers. He'd never been bullied in his life, and there was no way he'd suddenly become a target for bullying. Even if he had, I knew him well enough to know that his response wouldn't be to get himself transferred to another school.

"No, I wasn't," he agreed. "But I made everyone think I was. Look!" He pulled up his shirt, and I saw a bunch of nasty-looking bruises on his stomach. If I didn't know better, I'd have been really concerned, but I knew how easily he bruised. "Looks real bad, right? I gave Bruce McQueen all my holos to catch a suspension for this. Then I cried to my mom, she yelled at the principal, and bam! Goodbye Grove, hello Fitz. Admit it. You couldn't have planned it better."

He was right. It was a page right out of my book. My *old* book.

"You shouldn't have done that," I said between bites of my sandwich. I chewed and swallowed so I wouldn't spray bits of bread all over him when I said, "It was sneaky."

"Right, right, sure. So, what's the deal here?"

"The deal?" I said, playing dumb. It sounded unconvincing, even to me.

"The deal," he repeated. "Who's who? What's what? What are you running? How can I help?"

"I'm not running anything," I answered, completely truthfully this time.

"You're not—oh." He looked over both shoulders, then dropped to a whisper. "We can't talk here?"

"No. I mean, I'm not running anything. No plans. No side hustles. No cons. I don't do that anymore."

"DJ, come on. I'm not gonna snitch to your mom. Just tell me what—"

"Conor!" I hit the table so hard that the chocolate milk of the girl next to me almost tipped over. She glared at me and I shot her an apologetic glance before turning back to Conor. "I'm serious. I don't do that stuff anymore."

"You're telling me that you aren't planning anything? DJ, that's like saying you're a bird that doesn't fly anymore."

"So then I'm a penguin."

"No, you're not! You're an eagle. Or a raptor. Or a hawk. Something cool with wings that work. Not a dumb penguin that can't even fly! They're the penguins," he said, gesturing to the rest of the cafeteria.

"There's nothing wrong with being a penguin, Con.

Everyone loves penguins." He still didn't look convinced, and with our history, I didn't blame him. But I had to stick to my guns until he got the picture. I sighed. "Look, Conor. I get that you changed schools so we could hang out. And that's . . . that's wild, bro. That's some stuff that I would pull." He grinned like I had given him a compliment, which was not the reaction I wanted. I tried to make my face hard and serious.

"But I don't pull stunts like that anymore. The only thing I'm in charge of right now is my science class group project, and only because they made me. I don't plan things anymore. OK?"

He put his hands up. "Fine, fine. Whatever you say. You 'don't plan things anymore.' You're 'not like that.'" The air quotes he made were so aggressive it looked like his fingers might fall off. "That doesn't mean you don't know what's going on."

"I—"

"Ah-ah. Don't give me that, DJ. You can pretend to be a penguin all you want, but I know how your brain works." He tapped his forehead and then pointed at me. "Even if you're not trying to, all the wheels in there are spinning all the time."

I opened my mouth to argue, but he gave me a look that said he wasn't going to accept anything that I said besides the truth. I knew how persistent he could be, so I decided to save us both a pointless argument.

I tilted my head toward the table next to ours. "See the girl taking notes? That's Mariposa. She's the top guy's top guy. And she has a hookup in the front office. The secretary at the front desk is her aunt. But not a lot of people know, since they have different last names."

Conor nodded. "That makes sense, to recruit a number two with connections." He paused and giggled.

"What?"

"Number two."

I rolled my eyes. "Come on, man. We're in seventh grade. Grow up."

"All right, all right. I'm being serious. If she's the number two, who's the number one?"

"That would be Lucas. Goes by Lucky. White kid. Kinda chubby. Always wears a plaid shirt and a baseball cap indoors, even though it's against the rules. You'll know him when you see him. He has the look."

Con didn't need to ask what I meant by "the look." He was just as familiar as I was with the look of someone in their element. The look of someone who walked the halls like they owned them, because they more or less did. Honestly, most people can sense it, even if they can't put their finger on what they're sensing.

"Lucky. Got it. And what's his game?"

"A little of everything. He runs a lotto. He cornered the market on contraband snacks. Forges hall passes. He just started a video game tournament," I added, pointing again to the table that was deep in concentration, staring at their phones. "Plus, he takes a cut from everyone else who operates here. He's a good businessman. And a better enforcer. No one crosses him." I saw a spark in Con's eye that told me he'd heard my warning as a challenge.

"Conor," I said, narrowing my eyes at him.

He put up his hands like I'd attacked him. "Hey, don't look at me like that. I didn't say anything."

"You didn't have to," I shot back. "You know how my brain works. I know how yours works. I know what you just heard me say was 'It would be epic if we could figure out how to mess with the most dangerous kid at school,' but what you were supposed to hear was, 'It would be *the stupidest thing you've ever done* to try to mess with the most dangerous kid at school.'" I glanced over to Mariposa, nervous even though there was no way she could hear me over the noise. "You'd never get away with it."

"I could if you helped me." He leaned in close. "Come on, DJ. You know I'm right. You know you wanna come up with some awesome plan with tons of little details that I don't get until it's over and it worked and we're swimming in holos."

"Tickets," I said abruptly.

"What?"

"Tickets," I repeated. I needed to change the subject before he realized that his speech had been getting to me.

On my own, it was easy to pretend that I was fine with being a penguin, but you know what they say about birds of a feather. "No one trades holos here. They use tickets from the Starcade across the street."

"Hmm. All right. And the quickest way for me to get some would be—"

"I'm not helping you steal tickets, Con."

He made a huge huff. "Fine. What's the quickest *legit* way for me to get a lot of tickets?" He turned out his pockets. "You're not gonna let me walk around here flat broke, are you? And after I came all this way to see you."

From his voice I could tell that he was joking, but I still felt a little bad. He'd obviously put in a lot of effort to get his school changed just to get shut down by me. I suddenly remembered the brick of tickets in my pocket from Tyler and fished them out. "Here," I said, holding them out to Conor. "That's almost enough to enter the tournament. You play Rexcellent Racers, right? There's a big ticket prize for the winner."

Instead of taking the tickets, he just stared at me.

"What?"

"It's just funny."

"What's funny?"

"That, for such a good liar, you are a *terrible* liar, dude."

Just when I thought we'd gotten past that. I didn't know what else I could tell him to get him off my back. "I'm not lying to you."

"No. You're lying to yourself."

I rolled my eyes. "Don't give me that."

"No, I'm serious. In fact, if you can tell me one other thing you have going on here—one friend, one crew, one club—I promise I'll never bring it up again." He crossed his arms, daring me to lie to him.

"Uh . . ." I tried to keep my eyes from flicking around the way they did when I was grasping at straws.

"Well?" he pushed.

"I . . . uh, haven't really gotten into anything yet because I've been concentrating on school."

He scoffed. "You could sleep through your classes and still get straight As."

"Ah . . . yeah. Which is why . . ." As I scrounged for a good lie, my eyes landed on the bulletin board I'd passed before, and I felt my mouth open before I knew what I was saying. "Which is why I'm signing up for the school musical."

"Seriously?" Conor said.

Seriously? my brain said.

"Sure," I said. "It'll be fun. In fact, you should sign up too. Do something productive."

He made a face. "Hard pass." He paused like he was waiting for something. "Well?"

"Well, what?"

"You said you were going to sign up for the musical? Prove it. I saw the signup sheet when I walked in." He dug around in his pocket and came up with a pen. "I'll even let you borrow my pen."

He was playing chicken with me. Trying to call my bluff. *Fine*, I thought. Can't call a bluff if it isn't a bluff. I snatched the pen from him and marched over to the bulletin board. When I actually raised the pen to the page,

I hesitated for just a second, pen hovering over it without marking it. But I knew Conor was staring at my back, ready for me to chicken out, so I sucked it up and scribbled my name onto the next available line.

I marched back to the table, plopped back down into my seat, and slammed the pen down in front of Conor.

"There. Now get off my back, OK?"

"Sure," Conor said, before taking a long sip from his carton of chocolate milk. "Whatever you say."

Chapter Four
THE ITCH

After talking with Conor, I didn't have much of an appetite, so I made an appointment with David, my shrink. Well, technically, he's not my shrink. He's a peer counselor and he's only a grade ahead of me, but he wears a tweed jacket and wire-rimmed glasses to school. Most importantly, he takes confidentiality very seriously. It's why he was the only one at school who knew why I'd gotten myself transferred.

Or at least, he had been until Conor showed up.

"DJ," he said when he came to get me from the waiting area of the peer counseling classroom. It was set up almost like a real office, with a reception desk and two back offices that were used as private counseling and mediation rooms.

"I didn't think we had another appointment for a week."

"It's an emergency," I said, following him to one of the private rooms in the back.

"What do you mean?" As we walked in, he picked up a container full of lollipops and held it up. "Also, what flavor?"

"Double sour green apple."

He winced. "That bad?"

"Oh yeah."

"Then it's a good thing you stopped by." He gestured toward the couch that was set up opposite a worn armchair and waited for me to sit in it before he sat down across from me. Then he pulled a little notepad from his jacket pocket and crossed his legs. "OK. So, what's your emergency?"

"Do you remember how I told you about Conor? From my old school."

"I remember. Good friend, bad influence."

"Right, him. I just saw him."

"You mean, metaphorically."

"I mean, sitting across from me, in the cafeteria, eating fries. He got himself transferred. He goes here now."

"He—wait what? Transferred?"

I popped the lollipop into my mouth. "Yup."

"How?"

I shook my head. "You probably don't want to know." Confidentiality policy or no, I didn't want to burden him with Conor's shadiness too.

David took off his glasses and cleaned them on his shirt. Then, he dug around in the lollipop container until he found another double sour green apple, which he handed to me. "I think this is a two-lollipop kind of problem."

"At least," I agreed, tucking it into my pocket.

"OK, so if you don't want to say how, then what about why? Did he say why he got transferred?"

"He just said he missed me and he wanted to hang out at school again."

"Interesting. He didn't mention any specific . . . err . . . what terminology do you like?"

I snorted. "Scam? Job? Con? I don't care. It's the same

thing, no matter what you call it. And no. He didn't come to recruit me for a specific job. But, now that he's here, I know he wants to pick right back up where we left off. We talked for about five minutes and he was already juicing me for information on all the big players around here. It's only a matter of time before he tries to drag me into something."

"And how do you feel about that?"

I shot him a look. "Seriously, dude?"

He held up his hands apologetically. "I know, I know. But I have to ask it. It's on our checklist."

I huffed. "Yeah, I know. I guess I feel . . . worried."

"And why is that?"

"You know why."

"DJ—"

"I know, I know. It's on the checklist. I'm worried because . . . because I know that if he tries to bring me in on something concrete . . . I'll probably say yes." It was hard to admit to myself, even though I already knew it. I mean, it was why I had changed schools to begin with. It was why I'd ignored him all summer. "I *like* making plans. I *like* doing jobs. And I'm good at them. I've been trying to stay away from even being in charge of a class project that's too complicated, and then Conor shows up wanting to start up again? How am I supposed to handle that? I was so desperate to get away from him that I panicked and signed up for the school musical."

"Huh. You know, that's not a bad idea."

I couldn't remember having an idea. "What idea? Wait, you mean doing the musical?"

"Yeah. Why not?"

"How about I can't act, I can't sing, and I can't dance."

"I don't know about those last two, but everyone at this school thinks you're a loner nerd. Not a kid who might have gotten expelled if he'd ever gotten caught."

I grunted at him in response.

"Just think about it. The best way to take your mind off something is to think about something else. And you don't have to be in the musical. You could work behind the scenes. You know, props and logistical type stuff. Maybe that'll scratch the same itch."

I pulled the second lollipop out of my pocket and started unwrapping it. "Maybe. But that's not the only thing."

"What do you mean?"

"I mean, the reason I was thinking about the play in the first place . . . the only reason it was even on my radar is . . . Do you know Audrey Valentine?"

He raised his eyebrows. "*Oh.* It's *that* kind of thing."

"Don't say it like that."

"Sorry, sorry. You just usually don't want to talk about normal things that we have pamphlets for."

"I don't need a pamphlet," I said defensively. "I've just, you know, seen her around. And I think she might be cool to hang out with."

David stared at me. I stared back at him.

"Yeah, I'm gonna give you that pamphlet. But, hey. No judgment. This is a good thing. Normal, middle school problems. Not huge Machiavellian schemer problems. If you're concentrating on the play, you won't even think about Conor."

"You think so?"

"I do. But, just in case, we should go over the breathing exercises I showed you again."

We went over the breathing exercises, he gave me a pamphlet that I shoved to the bottom of my backpack, and then I went back to class.

I didn't see Conor for the rest of the day. It almost felt like I'd hallucinated the entire conversation. But, at the end of the day, my name was still on the signup sheet for the musical.

Kids were swarming the halls to get to the bus loop. I could follow them if I wanted to. Or, I could go to the music room where an info session for the musical was happening. My parents wouldn't be home for hours, so they wouldn't miss me if I walked home later.

On the other hand, I'd signed up for the musical, but no one knew that. They hadn't even collected the flyers yet. I could still cross my name out and not show up and no one would miss me. It was as simple as drawing a line across the page.

I pulled a pen out of my pocket, ready to do just that. But then I remembered the way Conor had looked at me when he'd said, "For such a good liar, you are a *terrible* liar, dude."

I shoved the pen back into my pocket and started walking toward the music room with determination. Determination that lasted about as long as it took for me to get within eyeshot. Once I saw that wide-open door, the courage left my body like water gushing out of a rain gutter, and I turned around, wondering if I could still catch the bus.

"Hey, wait!" said a voice from behind me, stopping me in my tracks. I recognized the voice. It was the same voice I'd heard singing the national anthem during the first pep rally of the school year. The same voice I occasionally caught snatches of when I walked past her locker, which was nowhere near mine or any of my classes.

When I turned, there was a girl standing next to the

music room door with reddish-brown hair that came down in waves and hazel eyes that were currently all big and excited.

"Are you looking for the meeting for the play?" she asked. "'Cause this is the right room."

"I, uh . . ." I could feel my determination dropping into negative numbers. I pointed toward the other side of the hallway, hoping I could make up for my suddenly stunted vocabulary with gestures. "Just, leaving. Uh, sorry."

I could feel my face burning up. Those weren't even real sentences! I had to get out of there before I made an even bigger fool of myself. I turned around and got about two steps forward before I felt her catch my wrist.

"Hey, hold on." She did a little skip hop so that she was standing in front of me again. "Were you thinking about signing up for the show?"

"I, uh . . ." Suddenly, I really wished I'd actually read David's pamphlet. "I was," I admitted, after trying and failing to come up with a better response than the truth. "But it was a dumb idea. It'll just be a waste of time.

I probably won't even get a part. You should go back in."

"What are you talking about?" she said before I could even try a third escape. "Didn't you read the flyers? Everyone gets a part. And, protip, not a lot of guys tend to sign up, so you'd probably get a good part if you stay. Oh!" She suddenly realized that she was still holding my wrist, something I'd been very aware of the entire time. "Sorry. I didn't mean to grab you like that when I don't even know your name. I just get excited. I should at least introduce myself before I start trying to sell you on joining the show, right?" She stuck out her hand for me to shake. "I'm Audrey."

"I know," I said, like an idiot, taking her hand. When she tilted her head at me in confusion, I quickly added, "I remember from when you sang at the pep rally. You were really good."

"Aww, thanks." She kept shaking my hand without letting go, looking into my eyes, questioningly. Were we having a moment? *No, you idiot,* said the tiny sliver of my brain that was still functioning properly. *You never gave her your name.*

"Oh! I'm DJ. Seventh grade. Just started here this year."

"Well, welcome to Fitz!" she said, ending the handshake naturally, as if I hadn't dragged it out for way too long. "I don't know if you've joined any clubs yet, but I can promise you, Drama Club is one of the best ones here. I love it."

"I can tell."

She grinned. "I know. I gush. Everyone says so. But I can't help it. My whole family is full of drama geeks. That's how I got my name. You know, from *Little Shop of Horrors*? My parents met at that show. If I was a boy, I would have been Seymour."

I remembered seeing the movie version of that musical on TV once. "Are you named after Audrey the girl or Audrey the man-eating plant?"

"Well, obviously the—" She stopped. "Huh. Actually, I never asked. That's a good question." She shrugged. "It's cool either way. They're both good parts. I'd be pumped to get either one. I mean, I know they say there are no small parts, only small actors, but sometimes you just really want one specific thing, you know?" Oh, I knew. "Like, in this play. *The Little Mermaid.* I know I'm only in seventh grade and the best parts almost always go to eighth graders, but I'm still going for it."

With her hair and voice and bubbly personality, I thought the director would be an idiot if they didn't cast her as Ariel. "I'm sure you'll get it," I said.

"I mean, fingers crossed, right? You haven't heard the other girls. Some of them are really good. But sometimes you have to just go for it, you know?"

She was looking directly into my eyes again. There was a good chance we really were actually having a moment this time. "Yeah. I think I do." Then I nodded toward the music room door. "Let's go."

Chapter Five
A SUMMONS

The rest of the week flew by. After the informational meeting for the show, there were still auditions. I spent all my spare time agonizing over which part to audition for. I knew that Prince Eric had a lot of scenes with Ariel and got with her at the end of the play, but I could barely talk to Audrey without getting nervous. What if I had to kiss her in front of people? That could be a disaster. Plus, I had that volcano project to do and that was keeping me pretty busy.

I saw Conor a few times during the week. At first, he kept trying to suck me into planning some kind of scheme or hustle, but when he realized I was actually busy and not just bluffing to get him to leave me alone, he seemed to back off a little bit to concentrate on the Rexcellent Racers tournament. Knowing Conor, he was just waiting for a better time to strike, but I still appreciated the break.

I finally decided on auditioning for Flounder, Ariel's sidekick. They still had a lot of scenes together, and hopefully, it would be less awkward than playing her love interest. I auditioned on Friday, finished the volcano stuff over the weekend, and came into school next Monday feeling pretty good.

The entire school was feeling pretty good, I think. We'd won our baseball game against the Timberwolves, with Tyler pulling off a final-inning home run. Everyone in science class was giving him little arm punches and congratulations. Even Mr. Conover mentioned it before he started his lesson on plate tectonics.

Tyler, for his part, handled the attention well. He only bragged about it in a jokey way, and he gave a lot of credit to the rest of the team. Before he sat down, he walked over to my side of the classroom and mouthed, "I owe you one," at me for forwarding him his part of the project over the weekend. Our presentation wasn't actually until the end of the week, but I thought I might as well get it done early.

It felt like one of those moments where the universe is conspiring with you instead of against you for once. And then, the PA system crackled on.

"Mr. Conover. Can you please send Darius James to the front office?"

Darius James. That was what I got called when I was in trouble. I stiffened as I tried to wrack my brain for a reason I could be getting called to the office. Since I'd been at the Fitz, I'd been squeaky clean. Maybe there was an innocent reason I was getting called in? Like maybe I'd lost something and they wanted to give it back to me? Or maybe I was getting an award.

Yeah right, I told myself as I took the hall pass from Mr. Conover and left for the front office.

I still hadn't thought of a good reason for me to have been called to the front office when I walked in.

Mrs. Delgado, the head receptionist, flagged me down as soon as she saw me.

"There you are," she said, before handing me a white envelope with *Darius James* printed on it in handwriting I didn't recognize. "This is for you."

"From who?" I asked, taking it from her.

"I don't know. Someone put it in my box between periods. Teachers do that sometimes when they're in a hurry."

I nodded, but I felt uneasy for some reason that I couldn't quite pin down. After you set up enough people, you can recognize a setup on instinct.

I slid my finger under the sealed envelope flaps and brought out the folded letter inside. It was more of a note, really, with only one short line: *Library. Third period. Don't be late.*

And, under that, instead of a signature, was a small doodle of a butterfly.

A chill ran down my spine. This wasn't a setup. This was a summons. I'd heard about it happening, but I never thought it would happen to me.

"Is Mariposa here today?" I asked, even though I already knew the answer.

"Mm-hm," said Mrs. Delgado. "She stopped by last period to say hi, actually. Are you two friends?"

"Something like that," I said, turning to leave. "Thanks, Mrs. Delgado."

Mariposa was Spanish for "butterfly." I was being summoned by Mariposa, which meant I was being summoned by Lucky, which meant I was in serious trouble and I had no idea why.

I opened the envelope wider, looking for anything else that might hold a clue as to why I was on his radar, but I didn't find one. I did find a hall pass though, for ten minutes into third period. It looked real, but I knew it had to be a very good forgery, signed by someone who knew how to fake the signature of the head receptionist.

By the time I got back to class, any high I'd been riding before was gone. Lucky didn't have chats with people. He had business meetings and he had inquisitions. And, as far as I knew, I didn't have any business with him. Unless this was about the work I did for Tyler. Could he want me to join his homework ring? I didn't think he was currently recruiting, but maybe one of his underlings had grown a conscience and he'd heard from Tyler I'd be a good replacement candidate.

I kicked myself mentally. I *knew* I shouldn't have taken those tickets from Tyler. I spent the rest of science class trying to think of a way to deny Lucky that wouldn't get me blacklisted, or worse, rocket boosted.

Next period, Duke was back in math class. Apparently, he'd watched *Monty Python and the Holy Grail* while he was out sick, and he wouldn't stop raising his hand to answer every question in this awful British accent. Under any other circumstances, I would have been glad to get away from him, but I would have put up with a whole seven periods of Duke's King Arthur impression if it meant skipping my library meeting. But I also knew that skipping the meeting would just make whatever was going on worse for me, so I flashed my hall pass and made my way to the library.

On the way there, I passed the peer counseling class-room and wondered if I should pop in for one last session before Lucky had my life ruined. But when I poked my head in, the waiting room was full, mostly with kids I didn't recognize. I did see that one giant kid I'd run into the other day though, and when he looked up, he saw me too. I quickly moved away from the doorway before he thought I was staring at him.

The Fitz's library was in the old part of the school. The ceilings tended to leak when it rained too hard, and the lights flickered at random. Some kids said it was haunted. I obviously didn't believe that, but it seemed like the kind of place that might be haunted, if that were a thing.

As soon as I walked in, I spotted Mariposa. It would have been hard not to. She was standing near the entrance, pretending to flip through a magazine that had just come in. When she saw me, she closed it abruptly and tilted her head toward the other side of the library, where the work-stations and tables were.

Everyone knew that Lucky didn't have gym because he

had a waiver to take an online health and physical education class instead. I didn't know how that worked exactly, but I did know that no other kid at school had managed to pull that off, and not for lack of trying.

So, instead of third-period gym, he had a free period in the library, which he was supposed to use to take his online class. But he just used it to conduct his business, which, today, included me.

When I rounded the corner, I saw Lucky sitting at one of the back tables, feet up. His baseball cap was on as always, and he had half a Twizzler hanging out of his mouth. The seat across from his was already pulled out for me. Mariposa, who had followed behind me, gave me a *Well?* kind of look, so I shuffled over.

"Darius James," he said, gesturing for me to sit down. "Twizzler?"

"No, thanks," I said as I sat. I didn't want to take anything from him unless I absolutely had to.

He snorted. "Relax. It's not poisoned. Besides, this is just a friendly chat."

A chat? Ha. I might as well have a chat with a dragon or Darth Vader.

"A chat about what?"

"A chat about you," he answered, pulling a manila file from under the table, which he opened and started reading from. "Darius James—"

"DJ," I corrected. It was a risk to interrupt him, but if I heard my full name one more time, I was going to lose it.

"DJ," he said obligingly. "Seventh grader. New at Ella Fitzgerald Middle School. Good grades. Really good grades." I wrinkled my nose. So this *was* about a homework ring. "Are you a smart kid, DJ?"

"I'm smart enough to know that this isn't a chat."

He chuckled. "You got me. He was right. You are smart."

I suppressed a sigh. This is what I got for doing Tyler a favor. I opened my mouth to try to politely cut the meeting short, when Lucky raised his hand.

"OK, smart guy. Let me read you a different file." He produced another folder from beneath the table. "Conor

Reed. Also new at Ella Fitzgerald Middle School. Middling grades."

"Conor?" I looked around, almost like I expected him to be in the room somewhere. "What did he do?"

"Ah, so you do know him."

I didn't want to give up more information than I had to before I knew what was happening. "I used to go to school with him. And now I do again."

"According to him, you used to do a lot more than just go to school with him. He told me a lot of stories that would be very impressive, assuming they're true."

I frowned. I'd kept my head down for months, and the second Conor showed up, he was out spilling my secrets. "Conor has a big mouth," I said. "I wouldn't believe everything he says."

"Hmm. Well, would you believe that he entered my Rexcellent tournament?"

"Sure," I said cautiously. "A lot of kids did." Where was this going?

"Sure, sure." He took a big chomp of his Twizzler.

"Would you believe that he not only qualified for the tournament, he made it to the semifinals? In fact, it looked like he might win the whole thing."

Looked. As in, past tense. As in, not anymore. "Well, that's not surprising. He's good at video games and tech stuff."

"Ha. Tech stuff. Mariposa?"

She came over and dropped her notebook in front of me. Inside was a list of names with a list of scores next to them. It was the same notebook I'd seen her writing in in the cafeteria. Conor's score was circled in red. "You see that? It's three times higher than anyone else's."

I didn't like where this was going. "Maybe he's just that good."

"Good enough to get zero derby car damage in every single round? I don't think so."

I gritted my teeth. I didn't need her to say another word for me to know what happened. But that didn't stop her from talking.

"When I started paying attention to his matches, really

paying attention, I noticed he wasn't taking any damage. Not only that, he never missed a turn. He always got the exact power-up he needed from item boxes."

How many times had I told Conor that less is more? How many times? But, apparently, without me to rein him in, he couldn't show any self-control.

"I had someone look into it, undercover," said Lucky, taking over narrating again. "Pretending to want to drop some serious tickets on whatever Conor was using to juice his performance."

I held my breath, even though I was already sure of the answer to my next question. "And he said?"

"He said that he didn't know what he was talking about, but to call him back when tourney season was over and he wasn't a potential competitor anymore. Which was as good as admitting he was cheating."

I let out all my breath in one, frustrated puff. "That idiot."

Lucky seemed caught off guard. He snorted. "Ha. Well, that answers the question of whether you were in it with him or not. Not that I thought you were. Smart guy like you."

I looked Lucky up and down. He looked relaxed. So did Mariposa when I checked on her. This didn't have the feel of people who were lulling someone into a false sense of security before a wild sucker punch. This really was as close to a casual chat as someone like Lucky was capable of having.

Which made me wonder why we were having it.

"I see that look," Lucky said, folding the last of his Twizzler into his mouth. "You wanna know why I dragged you out of math class to talk about something you didn't do."

"I mean, yeah. Not that I'm sad to get out of math class." I tried to keep my voice even. Keeping cool on the outside was always a good idea.

"Well, like I said, you can relax. You're not in trouble. Conor, on the other hand, needs to be rocket boosted."

"*What?*"

"Shh!" Mariposa said sharply.

"What?" I said again, more quietly. He wanted to rocket boost Conor? That was . . . OK, it was fair. I could admit that, looking at it from his point of view. New kid hasn't been on your turf for a month and he's already trying to cheat you out of money. What kind of message would it send to let him get away with it?

But people didn't get warned before they got rocket boosted. They were blindsided during the morning announcements like everyone else. And Lucky for sure didn't give a courtesy warning to their friends. The very fact that we were having the meeting had made me think that was off the table.

"If you've already decided on rocket boosting him—" Something clicked in my head. "You *haven't* decided on rocket boosting him. Not one hundred percent. Because . . ." Think. What would Conor do, caught and backed into a corner? "Because he made a deal. With you. Involving me."

Now Lucky smiled broadly. "Right again. Dang, DJ. Why haven't you been on my radar before today?" I gave a vague shrug. "Well, if you're as smart as you seem and as good as Conor made you sound, then maybe you can save your friend."

"That depends on what you want me to do."

"Well, I very generously offered your friend an out. I said that I could let him off the hook if he paid me the fifty thousand tickets he tried to cheat me out of, plus another fifty thousand, to prove he learned his lesson."

One hundred thousand tickets?

"One hundred thousand tickets?!" I hissed. "Are you crazy?" As soon as the words were out of my mouth, I remembered who I was talking to. Fortunately, Lucky didn't seem to notice my slipup. "He doesn't have that many. No one could get that many in a week."

"He seemed to think you could. I was so curious that I decided to call you in myself for a friendly chat. And to give you the chance to take me up on the offer. If you want to stake your rep that you can get me one hundred thousand tickets and risk the same punishment, I'll hold off on rocket boosting your friend for a full two weeks, to give you a chance to raise the tickets. If not, he's going down tomorrow."

I tried to keep my face even as I considered the offer. He was looking at me like he had X-ray vision and he was trying to look into my brain.

"Kids here don't keep that many tickets on hand. I couldn't get one hundred thousand tickets in two weeks unless I stole them from you—and that would kind of defeat the purpose, wouldn't it?"

"So you're saying you won't do it?"

"I'm saying I *can't* do it. Nobody could. It's impossible."

"Conor seemed pretty confident in your ability to do the impossible."

"I don't do the impossible."

"Don't or can't?"

When I didn't answer him, he said, "Well, like I said, I don't have any beef with you. You can go back to class."

"That's it?"

"That's it. You go back to your life. I go back to mine. And Conor . . . well, you know what happens to Conor.

Unless you change your mind before the morning announcements tomorrow."

"It'll still be impossible tomorrow."

Lucky smirked as he pulled out another Twizzler from his jacket pocket. "If it's impossible, it's impossible. Sorry for wasting your time. Mariposa?"

She gave me a look that told me I should leave.

So I did.

Chapter Six
ALARMING DEVELOPMENTS

I walked back to class, numb.

Even though I had understood every word Lucky had said to me, they didn't really register. It was like when you read a textbook about some historical event that happened two hundred years ago and you know it happened and you know it's important but you don't feel connected to it at all.

Conor had tried to scam Lucky, and in less than twenty-four hours, he was getting rocket boosted. Right, and the Declaration of Independence was signed in 1776. How long till lunch?

But then it was lunchtime, and when I saw Conor waiting for me at the entrance of the cafeteria, looking sheepish, everything hit me at once.

Conor had tried to scam Lucky, and in less than twenty-four hours, he was getting rocket boosted.

"There you are," he said, sounding relieved. "I—"

Before he could say another word, I hit him on the arm, as hard as I could.

"OW! The heck, man?"

"I told you one thing," I hissed at him. "One thing: Don't mess with Lucky. And what do you immediately do?"

"Look, it's not as bad as it—wait. How do you know what happened? I didn't tell you yet."

"HOW DO I—?" I realized we were still standing right where everyone was coming in and I was starting to yell, so I pulled Conor into a corner and tried again, more softly. "How do I know? Because Lucky got Mariposa to pull me from class so we could 'chat.' About *you*."

He grinned. "Oh, great. So you already sorted it out."

"Sorted it—how do you expect me to sort it out?"

"What type of question is that? You're DJ! You have connections! You sit down, have a chat, and you walk out, problem solved!"

"*Had.* I *had* connections at Grover. I'm no one here! I can't just snap my fingers and it's all good!"

He shrugged. "OK, so you make one of your plans and—"

"GAH! How many times do I have to tell you? I'm done with plans. I'm done with tricks. I'm done with bailing you out of trouble because you can't just cool it for *one week*."

He flinched a little at that before crossing his arms and taking a step back. "What? You're so mad at me that you're gonna keep pretending even when I'm in trouble?"

"You're only in trouble because you didn't listen to me! You *never* listen to me and then everything goes too far and then I'm changing schools because I feel so guilty that I can't walk through the front doors without wanting to puke!" I could feel my voice rising, but I didn't care. I was too upset. And based on the way his eyes were narrowed, he was just as upset.

"If you're gonna be like that, then I don't need your help. Maybe I should just get myself transferred back to our old school."

"Good! After you get rocket boosted tomorrow, you basically won't exist here anyway!"

A teacher dropped her hand between us, separating us. "Whoa, boys. What's happening here? Do I have to call someone?"

"No," I said, sending Conor a final, annoyed glare. "I'm leaving."

I started stalking off in the direction of my usual table, but by the time I got there, I realized that I wasn't hungry at all. Instead of sitting down, I got permission from one of the lunch monitors to go to the library instead. I needed to go somewhere quiet where I could be alone. I was so focused on my own problems on the way out that I walked right into some kid, accidentally pushing his lunch tray into his shirt. And it was sloppy joe day.

Before I could say anything, the kid mumbled out a "Sorry" and scurried away, like he was the one in the wrong. I stood there for a second, trying to figure out if I knew who the kid was, but I couldn't remember ever seeing him. It wasn't until I saw him turn toward the

Pluto table that I recognized him. It was Simon Pines.

Simon Pines, who I knew was at least a head taller than me, though you wouldn't have been able to tell it by the way he'd been walking, all hunched over and wearing his hoodie like it was a turtle's shell he could hide inside. He was the first kid who'd gotten rocket boosted after I started at the Fitz. One day, he'd been swaggering around like he owned the place, and then, bam. Two days before the October Monster Mash Dance, he'd gotten rocket boosted. Rumor was that he'd asked Mariposa to the dance and gotten rejected. When he started telling people that she still wet the bed, to retaliate, revenge had been swift and brutal.

Now, he mainly kept to himself, like all the other rocket-boosted kids. I hadn't realized how bad he'd gotten until I saw him sitting down, not even bothering to try to clean the soupy ground beef off his shirt. I shuddered. It was a messed-up thing to happen to a kid, even if he deserved it.

I tried to shake the image from my head, but when I

walked through the library double doors I was still thinking about it. I needed a distraction. Maybe they had some new comic books that I could throw myself into. I looked over toward the comic book shelf, and standing there, in his tweed jacket, holding an X-Men comic, was David.

I almost never saw him outside the office. It felt like some kind of sign.

"Hey, David."

He jumped and turned, like someone was out to get him. When he noticed it was me, he shoved the comic back on the shelf and snatched up his glasses from his pocket, shoving them onto his face.

"DJ," he said. "What are you doing here? Don't you have lunch this period?"

I made a face. "Yeah, but I wasn't feeling it. I . . . Actually, can you help me? I need some advice."

He looked over his shoulder, scratching his arm nervously. "I don't know. I'm not really supposed to give advice outside the office."

"It doesn't have to be official," I said. "Just one kid

talking to another kid who won't say anything because of their strong sense of personal responsibility."

David moved his mouth side to side, almost like he was swishing the idea around and seeing how it tasted. Finally, he said, "OK, fine. As long as it's nothing too—"

"How bad is it?" I blurted out.

"What?"

"Getting rocket boosted. How bad is it?"

His eyes went wide. "Rocket boosted? What do you—what did you—"

I quickly shook my head. "*I'm* not getting rocket boosted."

"But someone is. Who—" Something went off in his head. "Your friend?"

"It doesn't matter who. Just answer my question. How bad is it? I've seen kids that have gotten rocket boosted come to you for help."

"DJ, you know I can't tell you about what goes on in other people's sessions. It's confidential."

"I'm not asking you to spill anyone's secrets. I'm just

asking, in your professional opinion, how bad is getting rocket boosted, really?"

He took off his glasses and started cleaning them with the bottom part of his shirt. "It's . . . it's not good. I mean, look. If you're getting bullied, beat up, pushed around—that's bad. That's really bad. But you're still in the fight. You can push back. You can build your reputation back up. But when you get rocket boosted, it's like you don't exist. You're a ghost. You can't fight back when people don't even acknowledge you." He shook his head. "It's pretty much game over."

Game over.

I hadn't expected him to tell me it was all sunshine and rainbows—that was clearly not true—but the words still slapped me across the face.

I could still feel their sting the next day as I sat in homeroom, watching the morning announcements.

"Here's the lunch menu for today," said Lacey, one of the news anchors. "Popcorn chicken with a side of tater tots, green beans, or garlic bread. Milk. Chocolate milk. Strawberry milk. Skim milk."

While she was listing out every possible form of milk, Duke was drumming on his desk. Mr. Evans didn't even try to rein him in. We were only in homeroom for ten minutes, so I guess he figured it was best to wait him out until he was someone else's problem.

The loud, offbeat drumming wasn't enough to drive away the thoughts pounding in my head. Conor was going to get rocket boosted. Today.

"Two percent milk."

In the next few minutes.

"Almond milk."

Unless I did something about it.

"Duke," I hissed. He was drumming too loudly to hear me, so I jabbed him in the side with a pen. "Duke!"

"Wha—bro! You ruined my rhythm."

"Fifty tickets," I said hurriedly. "I'll give you fifty tickets if you run down to the library and open the emergency doors. *Now.*"

"Why do—"

"One hundred tickets."

"But you're not—"

"Five hundred."

"Sold. No take backs!" He was out the door so fast he almost left a cartoon smoke shadow. But was it fast enough?

"Thank you, Lacey," said Brad, the other anchor. "Now it's time for announcements." Any Rocket Booster announcements were always read right after the event announcements. I crossed my fingers under my desk that a lot of things were going on at school this week.

Duke had to run down the hall.

"Don't forget the canned food drive is ending this week."

Down a flight of stairs.

"There will be a Boy Scout meeting in the cafeteria after school."

Past the librarian and—

An earsplitting screech came in over the speakers. In the background, I could hear the alarm system going off, but over the mics it just sounded like feedback. The two kid anchors on-screen covered their ears and winced in pain.

"Turn it off," Brad moaned. "The alarm. It's too lou—"

The recording suddenly snapped off and was replaced with a "technical difficulty" graphic of a misfiring rocket.

I thunked my forehead onto my desk and took a breath. Hopefully, that would be enough to get Lucky's attention. I knew Lacey had to be on Lucky's payroll. He needed someone on the inside, and Lacey's big sister happened to be BFFs with Mariposa's big sister. I'd seen them talking in the parking lot more than once. And I noticed that she was always the one who read the Rocket Booster announcements. So it had to be her, which meant—

Which meant that Conor was right, I realized.

Not about trying to cross Lucky. That was still the dumbest possible move he could have made. But he was right about me. I *had* been storing up every little bit of information about the school's inner workings that I could. I *did* know what was going on. I could pretend to be a penguin all I wanted, but, at the end of the day, I knew that—

"DJ?"

I popped my head up. A runner from the front office was standing at the door, holding an envelope.

"He's right there," said Mr. Evans, pointing me out.

"Here you go," the runner said, handing me an envelope.

"Thanks." I waited for the runner to leave, checked to make sure no one was watching me, then opened the envelope.

Inside was a single notecard. On one side was a butterfly. And on the other were two words.

Two weeks.

Chapter Seven
A TRIP TO THE OCEAN

At lunch, I found Conor in the cafeteria surrounded by empty Fun Dip packages. His lips were stained blue and he wasn't even using the stick. He was just dumping the powder straight into his mouth and then licking the insides of the package. He looked rough, all glassy-eyed and robotic. I'd seen him cracking jokes when we were one wrong word away from getting expelled, so this was worrying.

He was so caught up in mainlining the sugar that he didn't notice I was standing right next to him until I said, "You got those from Choi, right?" He jumped, realized that it was me, and then went back to ripping the corner from another package of Fun Dip.

"They don't sell them in the vending machines," I continued, sitting next to him. "The PTA got them banned. You can only get them contraband, which I guess you already know. I'd stick to Choi. Royce sells just the powder for cheaper in ziplock bags, but everyone knows he mixes it with powdered sugar. And he's sloppy. People buying from him get busted by hall monitors at least twice as much. Most of them don't take bribes."

When he still didn't say anything to me, I stopped his hand before he could pour another half cup of pure sugar down his throat. "Conor, sugar isn't gonna make you less nervous. You're just gonna be bouncing off the walls *and* miserable."

He didn't look at me, but he opened his hand, letting the package drop. Dust spilled onto the table, which he tried to wipe up with his finger. I stopped him.

"Conor," I said sharply.

He finally twisted around to look at me. "Fine! You're right! You're always right! Is that why you're here? To say I told you so?"

I dropped his hand and scooted away from him a little to give him some space. "Whoa, bro. What happened between yesterday and today?"

"You wanna rub it in? Fine. I tried to be you. I tried to figure out a way out of this whole Lucky thing and . . . and no one will bite. You were right. He's untouchable. Everyone says you'd have to be stupid to mess with him. And I was bluffing. I can't just get transferred back, there's no way my mom will fall for that again. I . . ." He sighed. "I screwed up. This is why you always made the plans. I'm an idiot. And I'm gonna get destroyed. I would have gotten boosted today if that alarm hadn't gone off." He swiped up some of the blue powder with his thumb and licked it. "I'm a dead man walking."

"OK, first of all, don't eat off the table." I brushed the rest of the powder off. "It's gross. Second of all, that alarm didn't go off by accident. That was me."

He blinked at me. He blinked again. "That was . . . You set off the alarm?"

"Yes."

"*Why?*"

"Why? *Why?* Are you kidding me?" I flicked him on the ear. Hard. "Because we're best friends, *idiot.* You changed schools to chill with me even after I ignored you all summer. I can't just let you go down like this."

"But I thought you were mad at me."

"Not mad. Annoyed. If I was going to stop being friends with you just because you annoyed me, there's no way we'd still be friends. Besides, you were right."

He cocked his head. "No, I'm pretty sure I was wrong."

"Not about stealing from Lucky. That was just straight up dumb. I mean about me being a penguin. Or not being a penguin. *That's* why I was annoyed at you. Because I knew you were right. So when you got into this mess, I kind of exploded. I don't want to be like this, but I am. I'm a planner. That's just me."

"Wait." A slow smile crept onto Conor's face. "Does that mean you have a plan?"

"Ah, not exactly. I just got your rocket boosting

postponed for two weeks. Which means we have two weeks to figure out how to get Lucky one hundred thousand tickets, or both of us are going down."

"But you're going to think of a plan."

"I'm definitely going to try."

Conor grinned. "Yes! I'm sure that—"

I stopped him. "Hey, wait. Rules." I started listing off on my fingers. "We do this my way. I make all the calls. No one gets hurt. And, if I call it off, it's off. Got it?"

He nodded enthusiastically. "Yeah, yeah. Whatever you say. So, whose tickets are we taking?"

"Did you not just hear me—I said no one gets hurt!"

"Psh. But you don't have to hurt someone to take their tickets. Come on, even I know that."

He was right. There were tons of ways to get tickets from people without technically tricking them—a little persuasion and the right incentives can go a long way. But those methods involved more setup time than we had, and the Fitz was a pretty saturated market. Anything I did would be horning in on someone else's territory, and then we'd have another problem on our hands.

"I don't think we have enough time to raise the tickets properly," I said.

"Well, if we can't steal them and we can't raise them, then I dunno what that leaves us with."

He was right. It did limit our options. But not completely.

"Where do you get fish?" I asked.

Someone else might have looked at me like I was crazy, but Conor knew me well enough to know that I was going somewhere with it. "I dunno. The grocery store?"

"And where do they get the fish from?"

"The ocean, I guess."

I nodded. "Right. So let's go to the ocean."

As soon as school was over, Conor and I made a beeline for the Starcade, along with a stream of other kids looking to wash away the stress of the day, grab a slice of pizza, and maybe win some tickets. The second we walked in, we were hit with the one-two punch of the flashing, pinging game machines and the overpowering smell of baking pizza specifically designed to turn us into token-dropping zombies. On another day, it would have worked, but this wasn't a fun trip. This was business. And, before we took another step, I told Conor that.

"Hey," I said, stopping him at the door. "We're here for recon only, all right? No playing games. I mean, play the games, but it's just for research. No going rogue."

He nodded. "You're the boss, boss. Just tell me where you want me."

If I'd known there was an arcade recon mission in my future, I would have saved up some money for tokens. Luckily though, I had an ace in the hole: a Starcade coupon I'd gotten for getting the highest grade on our last math test. It was good for ten tokens and a personal pizza.

They said the pizza would be ready in half an hour, so I cashed in the tokens and split them with Conor.

"We'll divvy up the games," I said to Conor, handing him five tokens. "You take the right side. I'll take the left. Skip the games that don't give tickets and keep an eye out for anything that's paying out big time. We'll meet back up when the pizza is ready and report."

The first game on my side that I noticed was Skee-Ball. Even with all the newer, more high-tech games in the arcade, it was always packed with kids. When I walked up to the row of machines, all the lanes but one were filled with kids playing against their friends, side by side.

I snagged the last machine and slotted in a token. As I waited for the game balls to fall, I glanced up at the jackpot above the row of games. It had already climbed to two hundred tickets, but I'd seen it get up into the low nine hundreds.

I did some quick math in my head. I needed one hundred thousand tickets. If I was incredibly lucky and hit a nine-hundred-ticket jackpot every time—call it one thousand and be generous—that would still mean getting the money to buy one hundred tokens, which I just did not have. It would mean getting good enough at Skee-Ball to rack up the four-hundred-fifty-thousand-point total I needed every time. And, it didn't even take into account that the Skee-Ball jackpot reset to one hundred tickets every time someone broke the record.

By the time the balls crashed down to where I could reach them, I'd already nixed Skee-Ball from my list of viable games, but I still played out the round. Got twenty-two thousand points, a super-mediocre score. Even if I had all the tokens in the world, I'd run out of time trying to get the tickets that way.

Next I tried out the Whirlwind. It was one of those games where a light spun around and you had to try to stop it on a target to get a huge jackpot. The default jack-pot for the machine was five hundred tickets, and it got a lot higher than the Skee-Ball's jackpot.

There were four stations at the machine, and only one of them was already taken, by a girl with stringy blond hair and zoned-out gray eyes. I took the spot across from her and put in a token.

A blue light started to race around the machine. I let it loop for a few seconds to test its speed and then slammed down on the stop button. Too soon. I landed three spots shy of the jackpot window. A pathetic seven tickets spat out of the machine.

I pushed in another token and shook myself loose. That wasn't too bad for a first try. I should be able to hit it this time. I watched the light spin for another couple of seconds, resisted my natural urge to hit early and hit again. Late! I was one spot late!

Frustrated, I dropped another token. I had to get it this time. Lights. Spinning. Slam. Late by one again! When I reached for another token, I hit a lot more pocket than I expected before I hit the token—the last token, I realized. I'd wasted three tokens on one game. And I'd been worried about Conor messing around.

I ripped off my small string of tickets and shoved them into my pocket. Before I left, I stopped to watch the other kid at her end of the machine for a few plays. She was so laser focused on the light that she wasn't even looking up from the game machine to get tokens. She'd reach for her cup of tokens with one hand, drop one in, hit the button, and repeat. And every time she was one light short of the jackpot. I must have watched her play twenty rounds and she was one light short every time.

I shook my head. Rigged. I didn't know how, but it had to be rigged. I thought about saying something to the girl, but somehow, I didn't think she'd listen.

I was down to my last token, so I walked around for a bit, just scoping things out. There were some other land-on-the-target games that seemed more fair than the Whirlwind, but with payouts too low to make a dent in the one hundred thousand we needed. Same with the bank of shooting games. They were fine for fun or for making enough tickets to get by at school. Not enough to pay off Lucky though. I was halfway thinking about going back to the Whirlwind when I noticed something strange.

The middle school had just let out and the high school hadn't ended yet. At this point in the day, Starcade was usually pure kids my age. But sitting at a machine called Rowdy Roundup with a trash bag full of tickets spilling out of it was a guy who looked like he was in his late twenties. Maybe thirties.

Just like the girl at the Whirlwind machine, he was all concentration, but he had the tickets to show for it. I watched over his shoulder as he played. It looked like the point of the game was to corral farm animals as they dropped from the top of the screen into groups of three to make them disappear.

The guy kept clearing boards, but just barely. He kept missing obvious matches, letting the board almost fill up, and winning with a board-clearing lucky match at the last second. If he was making so many tickets playing like that, I was sure I could make more playing better. There was another Rowdy Roundup machine next to his, so I dropped in a token and started playing.

Once I got the hang of the controls, keeping the boards from overrunning with animals was a snap. I cleared the first few levels, easy. Things got a little tricky around level four and I finally crashed at level five. Not a perfect run, but I'd gotten a lot further a lot faster than the other guy. So I was a little surprised that, even with all the flashing and congratulating my machine was doing, it only paid out ten tickets.

It had to be broken, right? Or maybe his machine was. Why else would this guy who was barely making it out of every level be cleaning up while I was making next to nothing?

The pop rock blaring from the speakers paused and a man's voice said, "DJ, your pizza is ready."

Good timing. I made my way over to the pizza counter and sent Conor to snag a table when I ran into him. Then, I gave him a slice of pizza and let him eat while I gave my report.

Unfortunately, he didn't have better news than I did.

"I got nothing, man," he said. "I tried hoops, one of the racing games, a whack-a-mole type thing where you have to stomp bugs. This is all I won." He dumped a few strings of tickets on the table. It would have been a respectable pile if not for the circumstances. "I'm not the math guy but even I know that's not enough."

"No, it's not." I sighed and bit into my slice of pizza. "And when I saw the guy with that huge trash bag of tickets, I really thought . . ."

The words coming out of my mouth trailed to a stop but I barely noticed because my brain had suddenly kicked into overdrive. It couldn't be that easy, right? And they had to have safeguards up. But, then again, I'd never noticed any. And would you put up safeguards for something you didn't realize anyone would do?

Conor waited for a second before waving his hand in front of my face. "You thought what? If you're gonna zone out, you gotta take me with."

"OK, OK. Listen. You win the tickets. Then you put them through the ticket counter, right? Then what?"

"Oh. Oh! The trash!"

I shushed him. "Not so loud." I looked around to see if anyone was paying attention to us, but no one was. "All right. New plan. We walk out of here, nice and slow. Then, we head out back to the dumpster and one of us checks it out while the other keeps watch."

He agreed and I finished my pizza. Then, as casually as we could, we slunk out the front doors and moseyed over to the dumpster behind the building.

"Ugh," Conor said as we got close. "It smells like a pizza threw up."

"Well, get over it and get in that dumpster."

He made a face. "Why do I have to go in the dumpster?"

"Which one of us tried to cheat Lucky again?"

"Getting in the dumpster."

I gave him a boost and then checked the corner. No one was anywhere near us. Things were looking up.

"Oh no."

I whipped back around to check on Conor. "What is it?"

"Look." He held up a clear plastic bag full of tickets. Shredded tickets. "The ticket-counter machines must shred them when they count them."

I blinked. I blinked again. So close again and then a monkey wrench. And I'd been so hopeful this time. "Gah! I . . . Are you sure they're all shredded?"

"Yeah, man," he said. "All these bags are . . . wait."

I could feel my heart jump in my chest. "Wait what? Wait, you saw a rat? Wait, someone's coming? Wait—"

"Tickets!" he said triumphantly, holding up a bag of unshredded tickets. "Ones we can use!"

"Shh! I mean, yes! But shh!" I helped him down from the dumpster and looked at the tickets. Now that I was up close, I could see that some of them were partially shredded and they smelled awful, but about half the bag was full of intact tickets. And the bag was stuffed. More stuffed than the bag of the dude who was playing Rowdy Roundup. There had to be close to ten thousand tickets in there. "This is crazy! This is amazing! This is . . . this is too good to be true."

"How?" Conor asked.

"I don't know, but it is. This feels too easy."

He scoffed. "You try climbing into a dumpster and then tell me how easy it is."

"OK, fine. But maybe these won't work since they've been in the machine already."

"Doubt it," said Conor.

"Why?"

"Because why would they go through the trouble to shred them if they couldn't be reused?"

It almost annoyed me when Conor had a good thought because it reminded me that he had a brain—he just chose not to use it 99 percent of the time.

"Here," he said, reaching into the bag and ripping off a string of tickets. "I'll go in and test these out. If they work, we know we're good."

"Conor, wait. We should—" But he was already gone.

My brain started going into overdrive again, but this time, it was working against me. What if this was a trap? What if Conor got caught? What if we got detention? What if we went to jail? What if—?

"Check it, DJ!"

And, when I looked up, Conor was rounding the corner, proudly holding up a receipt from the ticket counter. When he got closer, I could see that it read *Starcade Winner's Receipt *29 Tickets**

Nothing extra. Nothing suspicious. Nothing to suggest he got the tickets from a dumpster instead of winning them.

I took the receipt from his hands, held it up to my eyes, and breathed deeply. Then I handed it back to him and nodded.

"All right. Now we're in business."

Chapter Eight
A SLIGHT PROBLEM

The first thing we had to do with the tickets was launder them. And I don't mean like how criminals launder money so it looks like they got it from a legit source. I mean literally running the tickets through the dryer with a huge spray of Febreze. The machines might not have been able to tell that the tickets were dumpster tickets, but anyone with a working nose would be able to put two and two together if we came in with an entire pile of them.

After that, we came up with a system. We'd split the tickets between us and stick them in our backpacks. Then, after school, we'd go to the Starcade and run them through the machines. Once we got our receipts, we'd check that the coast was clear, go to the dumpster, and grab another bag of tickets. We'd go home, clean them, sort out the ones we could use, and repeat. It was simple, clean, and worked perfectly.

For exactly one day.

When school ended on Wednesday we headed to the Starcade with our split load of tickets to start raking in the tickets. Conor and I started out at machines that were side by side, but I decided to switch to a machine on the other side of the floor to be safe. Two high rollers were more likely to be noticed than one. I knew I was being a little paranoid, but paranoia has saved my butt more than a few times.

The ticket machine on the other side looked a little different than the one I'd been using—it didn't have the Starcade logo on it—but it worked the same. I took a knee and started feeding tickets into the machine as quickly as possible. The less time I spent there, the less suspicious it would look to anyone paying attention.

I was about a third of the way through the tickets when I heard a voice from behind me.

"Wow. How'd you swing that?"

My soul left my body for a second, but I didn't let it show. Jumpy insides, calm outsides. That's how you stay in control.

When I turned around, I recognized the guy instantly, even though I'd never talked to him. It was the guy I'd seen playing Rowdy Roundup. From what I could tell based on how chummy he was with the staff, he was there every day right around when school was finishing for us. And he wasn't just good at that game. I'd seen him killing it on about four other games too.

I did a quick scan of his face to see if he looked like he was suspicious of where I'd gotten the tickets, but, as far as I could tell, he was just curious.

I faked a casual shrug. "Just lucky, I guess."

He chuckled. "Ha. We all have our methods. I get it. But lemme know if you wanna swap tips. We APs gotta stick together."

"Uh-huh," I said, not knowing what I was agreeing with at all.

"Dang," he said. "You guys get younger all the time. There was this other kid, but he was a little older and he moved. Good time to get into the game though. It's about to get a lot less annoying."

"What do you mean?"

"You haven't heard?" He slapped the top of the machine I was using. "These are going away."

My soul left my body for the second time in two minutes.

"What do you mean they're going away?" What were they going to do? Count the tickets by hand?

"I mean these janky ticket counters." He gestured to the one I was using. "They're starting a huge remodel next Wednesday and they're replacing the old ticket counters. The new ones are supposed to run a lot smoother and the ticket shredder part doesn't jam as much."

Next week Wednesday? That was almost a week before our time to pay Lucky back was up. At the rate we were going, we'd only have about half the tickets we needed by then.

My brain was slamming down on the hyperventilate button, but I just took a quick breath. Jumpy insides, calm outsides.

"That definitely sounds more convenient." For everyone but me.

We chatted for a little bit longer before he went off to do something else. Then, as soon as he was gone, I hightailed it over to Conor.

"Conor," I hissed.

"Hey, man," he said, without turning. "You done already?"

"No. But we need to talk. We have a *situation*."

Now he turned around. "What do you mean, situation?"

"I mean we can finish this later. We need to talk now."

I pulled Conor to the back of the building. During work hours, there was rarely anyone back there.

"OK, we're alone. What's going on?"

"Our operation is in trouble," I said, before telling him what the other player had told me. "I did the math," I finished. "Even if there's a bump over the weekend with kids being out of school, we won't be able to get what we need."

"Are you sure?"

"Am I sure? About *math*?"

"OK, OK, I'm sure you're sure. Right, cool. Awesome." Conor clapped his hands together in a way that made it clear that he did not believe our situation was cool or awesome. "OK, wait. We're going to have more than half of what we need. Maybe if we give him that, Lucky will go easy on us?"

I shook my head. "Lucky doesn't do easy. If he did, he wouldn't be Lucky."

"All right. All right. OK, so can we raise the other forty-thousand-ish tickets another way in the six days we have left?"

"Maybe, but I doubt it. Forty K sounds easy next to a hundred K but that's just because a hundred K was double impossible. This is just regular impossible."

Conor kicked the wall. He's more of a jumpy insides, jumpy outsides kind of person. "Great. Great! We're sunk!"

I smacked the back of his head. "Calm down! You know, you get really hysterical for a guy who's in trouble so much."

"Yeah, trouble I can get out of. That's different. Unless you figured out some genius plan to get us out of this in the past thirty seconds."

Unfortunately, I hadn't, and it wasn't for lack of trying. My brain had been chasing its tail trying to figure out a solution since I'd realized our plan had hit a roadblock, but so far, I had nothing.

"I haven't," I admitted. "But we still have time. Hey, I didn't even think we'd get this far, so let's not give up yet. And let's keep getting tickets this way as long as we can. Then, we only have to figure out how to get our hands on the last forty K."

He looked skeptical, but he nodded. "You're still the boss, boss."

I rolled the problem around in my head for the rest of the day, but I didn't come up with anything.

I was still thinking about it the next day as I stood in

line for lunch. I picked up my chicken nuggets and swiped my card.

When I trudged to my seat, Conor was waiting for me.

"Anything?" he asked.

I shook my head. "My brain is a blank. Crazy, I know. But it is." I sighed and wondered if David had any appointments open for today. "I can't think of a way around it. We need a big score. I mean a *huge* score, all at once. But the Starcade just doesn't have that kind of capacity."

Conor stopped loudly slurping juice through a straw and said, "What if it was a different Starcade?"

"What?"

"What if it was a different Starcade?" he repeated. "A bigger one. More people. More tickets."

"I—huh." I scratched my head. "That would . . . I mean . . . yeah, but . . . huh." Another Starcade. A *bigger* Starcade. A bigger score. I hadn't thought of that, but he was right, at least in theory.

"I was just thinking, because there's the big Mega Starcade way across town, right?"

I'd only been to the Starcade he was talking about once. If our Starcade was a slot machine at a convenience store, that one was Vegas. Just all of Vegas. Everything was bigger. Crazier. More machines. Bigger prizes. Even a huge tunnel system in the ceiling for kids to play in. It was awesome.

But it was also forty-five minutes away.

"My parents would never drive me that far to go to an arcade when there's one literally across the street from school. And neither would yours. They'd say it was a waste of time and gas." The crowd of kids watching the Rexcellent tournament suddenly cheered. They were really having a party over there. I was half surprised a lunch monitor hadn't shut them down yet.

Wait.

Party.

Starcades threw birthday parties. I wouldn't be able to get my parents to drive me to the far Starcade just because, but if there was a birthday party . . .

"What?" Conor demanded. "I see that face. What are you thinking? You have an idea."

"Barely an idea. Half an idea. More like the skeleton of an idea."

"Dude, just tell me. I can't help you fix it if I don't know what it is."

He had a point. "OK, but I'm telling you up front, I have no idea how to make this work. You know how Starcades have birthday packages? What if we got ourselves invited to a party at the Mega Starcade?"

He perked up. "Hey, you're right. My mom would probably be cool with that. But who's having a party there?"

"No one that I know of," I said. "And they probably wouldn't invite us since you're new and I don't really have any friends here besides you. And we don't know the setup of the building, since we haven't been there since the second grade. And you know I don't run jobs this big without a full crew. All we have are the Brains—me—and the Fingers—you. We don't have a Face or Muscles."

He deflated slightly, but only slightly. "OK, sure, but at least that's a list, right? A list of things to figure out is better than a blank brain, right?"

"I guess." A death-trap obstacle course was better than a gaping chasm, but not by much. "I'll keep thinking about it. Meet you out front after school?"

"Cool."

For the rest of the day, I worked the idea around in my head like Play-Doh. Tweaking details, looking for answers, tallying up my resources. But I still kept running into the same problem. I didn't have a crew here. It was just me and Conor.

And don't get me wrong. Conor is great. But he's not a full crew. He's the Fingers. He's good at grabbing things without being noticed and at electronics. Swiping and typing. He's got his specialties and he basically sticks to them. Same as me. I'm the Brains. I make plans. I oversee. We're not intimidating enough to be Muscle or charismatic enough to be Faces. And I didn't see how any plan I could come up with would work without those roles filled.

After the final bell rang, I hurried to the front of the school to meet up with Conor, but a few steps from exiting, someone pulled on my sleeve.

"DJ!" When I turned, I saw Audrey behind me. She was bursting with excitement. "Hey! Where are you going? Have you checked the cast list yet?"

I'd completely forgotten that roles for the show were being announced today.

"Right, I was about to check on that," I lied, badly. "But what about you? Did you get your part?"

She shook her head with a good-natured smile. "Nah. Brianna Williams did. But she's an eighth grader and they get priority. I still have another year. Plus, she's really good. I'm happy for her."

"Yeah, well, I think you would have made a really good Ariel."

She frowned in confusion. "Ariel? I didn't try out for Ariel. Oh, Hailey Coombs got Ariel, by the way. No big surprise."

It was to me. I thought back to our earlier conversation and realized she'd never actually said she was trying out for Ariel. She said she was going for the best part. "Well, if you didn't try out for Ariel, who did you try out for?"

"Ursula."

"Ursula?! Isn't Ariel the best role in *The Little Mermaid*? I mean . . . she's the little mermaid. And Ursula is the bad guy."

She nodded. "Yeah. That's why I wanted it. She gets to sing that cool, dark song and strut around the stage." She put on a frosty glare and circled me with measured, intimidating steps that made her seem a foot taller before shrinking back to her normal tiny self with her usual grin. "It's so much fun. And I like getting to play a role that's different from who I am. That's the whole point of acting, right . . . ? Right? DJ, you're staring off into space. Are you OK?"

"Yeah," I finally said. "I'm fine."

Better than fine. Maybe one of the puzzle pieces I needed was already right in front of me.

"Hey, Audrey," I said. "This is going to sound weird, but I might have a better role for you."

Chapter Nine
THE FACE

Conor wasn't on board with letting Audrey in on the job at first.

"The girl from the show?" he asked as we waited for her outside the school. Audrey was still in the building, getting her things. I'd promised to explain what I meant about a better role on the way to the Starcade. "You barely know her and you trust her to be our Face?"

"I'm telling you," I insisted. "Just now, in there, when she was pretending to be Ursula—it was like she was a completely different person. And she was just messing around. She could be as good as any Face we've ever worked with."

"That doesn't mean she'll work with us," Conor

shot back. "Even if she's the best actress in the world, it doesn't mean she'll help us once she knows what we're doing."

"Well, if she says no, we're not any worse off than when we started, right?" That wasn't necessarily true. She could rat us out to the arcade or our parents or another industrious duo of kids who wanted to make a quick couple of tickets, and then things would be way worse. But I was willing to take the risk.

After a few minutes, Audrey came out of the school, spotted us, and waved excitedly. When I waved back, Conor groaned.

"What?" I said, through my teeth so she wouldn't see the smile slip from my face.

"That's her? She looks like she might have My Little Ponies in her backpack right now. She looks like she would cry if my little sister looked at her too hard, and my little sister is three. She looks like—"

I shushed him quickly as Audrey came within earshot.

"Sorry, sorry," she said, running up. "I had to get some

books for my homework. Oh! We haven't met! Hi, I'm Audrey."

"Conor."

"He's the friend I was talking about." I picked up my backpack and slung it over my shoulder. "Come on, we should get going."

As Audrey fell into lockstep next to me she said, "So, what were you talking about before? About a role? Is this for, like, a play or something?"

I glanced over at Conor and he shrugged at me. On my own. Fine. It was what I'd expected anyway. Well, better to ease her in.

"How much do you know about school politics?"

She scrunched up her face all puppy-like. "You mean like class president and stuff?"

Conor was giving me a look that said, *She's useless! Cut her loose!*

I ignored him. "Uh, no. I mean like real power. Choi's sugar cartel. Simone's homework racket. Lucky's iron grip on the student body."

She shrugged lightly. "I mean, I know that stuff happens. I don't really get involved though."

Behind her back, Conor threw up both his hands like *See? Are we done now?* I ignored him a second time.

"Yeah, I was trying to stay out of it too. But that one—" I pointed at Conor, and he stopped waving his arms around like he was trying to land an airplane before Audrey looked back at him. "That one ended up in debt to Lucky. Long story. Big debt. Really big debt. One hundred thousand tickets' worth of debt."

Her eyes widened. "Oof. Lucky doesn't let anyone cross him. If he came after me, I don't know what I'd do."

"There's only one thing we can do," I said. "Raise the tickets. And it's going OK. But our time limit is coming up, so we need to take some drastic measures or we are both going to be rocket boosted and then it's game over."

"That's terrible. But I don't know how I can help you with that. Or what it has to do with acting."

"It's more, uh, acting adjacent. But first, we have to pick something up at the Starcade." We crossed the street and Audrey started going for the front door. I stopped her.

"I thought we were going here," she said.

"We are," said Conor. "But we're not going in." We'd decided before she'd come out. It broke our system, but she needed to see it.

When Audrey looked at me questioningly, I said, "Audrey? We're going to let you in on something. Something major. And, if you don't want to help us out after that, then it's OK. But you can't tell anyone what we're doing, all right? It would ruin everything. You got that? Can we trust you?"

"Yeah," she said easily, like she didn't even think about it. "But I still don't get what's going on."

"You will," I said. "Come on."

We led her around to the back of the building where the dumpsters were.

"What are we doing back here?" she asked.

"I figured out something about the ticket-counter machines," I said. "Usually, they shred the tickets when they count them. But sometimes the machines don't work right. So the tickets go through and come out mostly intact. And then they just throw them away with the shredded ones."

As I was talking, Conor was already scrambling up to the top of the dumpster to scope out the trash bags. Once we'd started raking in the tickets, he'd gotten over his squeamishness pretty quickly.

Audrey squinted at him and then at me. "Wait, what?"

I walked over to the side so I could keep watch, and she followed me. "We have to pay Lucky one hundred thousand tickets. Do you know how much that is? Most kids don't see that many in their entire three years at the Fitz, and he wants that many in two weeks."

"So you're stealing them from the dumpster?"

"Not stealing," I corrected. "It's not stealing if it's from the trash. I checked." Whether or not it was trespassing was a legal gray area, but I was trying not to think about it too much.

"I guess. But it's still weird."

"I know. I wouldn't usually do this sort of thing." At

least not in the extremely recent past. "But Conor and I go way back. You get it, right? Getting your hands a little dirty to help a friend?"

"You're not the one getting your hands dirty," Conor grumbled as he shuffled through the trash. I guess he hadn't got over his squeamishness entirely.

"Anyway, we don't want you to dig through trash. We just wanted to show you what we were doing, so you would know the full story before you made a decision. We wanted you to trust us."

She rubbed her shoulder uncomfortably. "I don't know. This feels weird. And I still don't get why you need me."

"You heard her," Conor said from the trash. "She's out. Let's find someone else."

"Give her a break," I said. "She doesn't even know what's happening yet."

"And she's already spooked. She can't do it."

"Do what?" asked Audrey.

"Yeah, she can. And she's not spooked, she's confused."

"Confused about what?" asked Audrey.

"Face it," said Conor as he hopped down with a full bag of partially shredded tickets. "You either have it or you don't. And she doesn't."

"Have *what*?!"

"What are you kids doing out here?"

The middle-aged manager of the Starcade suddenly swung open the side door, holding a bag of trash. He scanned us suspiciously, and we froze—Conor holding the bag of tickets, me with Audrey, trying to keep her calm.

Well, I say *we* froze. I mean Conor and I froze.

Audrey burst into tears and ran up to the man.

"Oh great," Conor mumbled under his breath, shooting me a dirty look. I held up a hand to him apologetically. Bringing in a new person was always risky. I knew that. But I'd been so sure about her. And now she was cracking under the slightest bit of pressure.

"We're never going to find them!" she wailed.

"Find what?" the man asked—which was the same question I had.

"My earrings!" Audrey sobbed, burying her head in her hands. "My mom got them for me last Christmas and I know I had them when I got here, but I don't know what happened. Look, they're gone!" She tugged on her earlobes to show she wasn't wearing any. Which was weird because I could have sworn she had been before. "They were helping me look for them. I thought maybe they got tossed in the trash accidentally, but it's no use! I'll never see them again."

As she cried, the man looked like he wished he had sent someone else to take out the trash. "Er . . . that's too bad. Why don't you—uh, if you tell me what they look like, we can keep a lookout for them."

She shook her head miserably. "No, it's all right. I probably didn't even lose them here. I probably lost them at school and didn't realize until I got here." She sighed. "Mom is going to be so disappointed in me."

The manager dug through the pockets of his khakis until he came up with a creased piece of paper. "Um, this isn't much, but you can use this to get an ice cream cone, on the house. I, uh, hope you find your earrings." Then, he shuffled back into the Starcade awkwardly, still holding the trash bag.

As soon as the door was shut, Audrey turned back to us, dry-eyed as before. "We should go before he comes back with more questions."

We were still standing there in surprise when she pulled her hoops out of her jacket pocket and started putting them back in. "Come on! And grab that bag of tickets if you want them. I live just down the street. This way."

When she moved, we finally snapped out of it to follow her.

"She can cry on command?" Conor hissed at me, softly enough so she couldn't hear. "Why didn't you say so?"

"I didn't know! But did you see that? That was a perfect Crybaby with no prep. I told you. We need her."

"Well, I believe you *now!*"

Audrey's house was as close as she'd said. We were there within minutes.

"My parents won't be home for a few hours," she said. She let us in through the back door so we could leave the trash bag on the back porch. She threw her backpack on the couch and went toward the kitchen. "Do you guys want cookies or juice or anything?"

"What I want is to know where the heck that came from?" Conor said.

"The juice?" she said, cocking her head to the side. She was all confused puppy again, like she hadn't just burst into tears at the drop of a hat.

"Not the juice! You just turned on the waterworks and totally played that dude! I thought we were gonna get in trouble. Instead, we got free ice cream."

She shrugged. "Oh, that's no big deal. No one likes being in the room with a crying girl. You can basically get out of anything. Everyone knows that."

"But not everyone can pull it off like you did," I said. "You're a natural. You had a story. You had the tears. I didn't even see you take your earrings off."

"It was when she put her head in her hands," said

Conor. "It was really quick, but I saw it. She's done it before, I bet."

"Once or twice," she admitted. "But just to get out of little things." She came over to where we were on the couch, balancing a plate of chocolate chip cookies and a huge glass of milk.

"Well, you're good," said Conor. "Really good. And you can believe me because I didn't even want you on the team at all ten minutes ago."

"The team for what? I'm still really confused about what's going on here. Can you just explain it with details? And stop talking about me like I'm not in the room."

I glanced over at Conor, whose mouth was already crammed with cookies. This time, his face was saying, *Tell her already!* Audrey had sat down on the carpet, cross-legged, and looked up at me, waiting.

"All right. Here it is. Our plan was to keep collecting tickets from the trash, but there's going to be this remodel next week at all the stores. They're getting rid of the old ticket-counter machines, and the new ones shred better.

We're going to be short about a third of the tickets we need, and our Starcade is too small. They don't throw enough tickets away every day. But we came up with a plan. The only thing is, we need someone who can do what you do to make it work. Someone who's good with people. With emotions."

"A Face," said Conor.

"An actress," I covered quickly. If we started throwing around terminology like that, we were going to sound like career criminals. Which wasn't a completely unfair way to describe us, but I was trying to make a good impression. "We need an actress. And when you told me you liked playing bad guys . . . Audrey, whatever part you're playing in the show, this is better. I promise. You get to be the lead. You get to improvise."

"And is it bad? Or wrong? Or illegal? I like to play bad. I don't want to actually *do* anything bad."

"We're on the same page," I said. "That's why we're getting the tickets out of the trash. We're not taking them from people who'll miss them. We're taking what's been thrown away. Oh, and there's tickets in it for you. You can have everything we don't need to pay off Lucky."

"Ehwywing?" Conor said, through his full mouth.

I shushed him. "No pressure, but I don't think we can do this without you. It's a good plan, but it won't work without all the parts."

Conor swallowed with a huge gulp. "At least hear him out. It's a really cool plan. It should have, like, theme music."

"That cool?" she said, with a small laugh.

"You know, I do what I can."

"Well, then." She took a bite out of her cookie. "I better hear this plan. Walk me through it."

Chapter Ten
THE HOOK

"The actual plan is simple," I said, once I explained our laundering system. "There's not enough tickets at the nearby Starcade, so we want to do the exact same thing but on a bigger scale at the Mega Starcade across town. One big score in one day should be enough."

"The hard part is getting to the arcade," Conor chimed in. "It's really far. Our parents would never drive us there in the middle of the week, especially when there's a Starcade in town. It would have to be a better reason than us just wanting to go."

"Like a birthday party. I know my parents would take me if there was a party there and I was invited. They want to make sure I make friends."

"Same," said Conor.

"That makes sense. But do you know anyone who's having a party there in the next week?"

"No. That's why this is the hard part. We need to convince someone to throw a party at the Mega Starcade before the remodel next Wednesday, *and* get invited to the party."

"You're right," Audrey said. "This *is* harder than pulling trash out of a dumpster."

"I went online and grabbed as many birthdays for kids at school as I could find," Conor said, pulling a list out of his backpack to show Audrey. "I got twenty-one kids with birthdays in the next week. A few from each grade."

"It needs to be someone you know," I said as she glanced over the list. "Someone who we can convince to do a Starcade party. Someone whose parents will pay for it on short notice. Someone who—"

"Ariel," Audrey said suddenly.

"Huh?" Conor leaned over so he could read the list over her shoulder. "There's no Ariel on here."

"No. I mean the girl playing Ariel in the show. Hailey Coombs, remember? She's on the list. And we're friends. Not best friends, but I'm playing one of her sisters in the show and we were both in the school play last year too."

"OK," I said. "Good. Possible targ—I mean, option. Does she like Starcade? Would her parents give her a Starcade party?"

"Her parents would give her whatever she wanted. Last year she left class for her entire birthday week and went to London with her mom. The thing is, I don't think she likes Starcade that much. With her parents' money she could go as much as she wanted, but she almost never does."

"So we have to figure out a way to make her want it," I said. "But not in an obvious way. She has to think she came up with the idea on her own. No one likes being told what to do. Can you think of any reason she would want to go to the Starcade?"

"Hmm." Audrey rubbed her face thoughtfully. "I don't know. She's really not the—wait, Tyler."

"Tyler?"

"Tyler Monroe," she confirmed, as if Perfect Tyler needed last name confirmation. "She *loves* him. If throwing a Starcade party meant Tyler would show up, she would for sure have a party there."

"Oh, dude, that's perfect," Conor said. "Don't you have the hookup with him?"

"I didn't know you and Tyler were friends," Audrey said.

"We're not," I said, cuffing Conor on the shoulder. "Conor just has a big mouth. That's why we're in this mess. But I don't think it should be a hard sell. We have science together, and he probably likes Starcade as much as the next guy. The trick is gonna be the timing. Do you know what classes Hailey has for second and third period?"

"Umm, history with Mr. Lewis for second. And then English I think? With Ms. Jacobs?"

I made a face. "No good. Those are both on the other side of the campus. There's no way we can accidentally, on purpose, run into her. Hmm . . . unless." I grabbed a notebook and pencil from my backpack and started sketching out the layout of the campus. "This is where I'll be, with Tyler at the end of second period. This is Ms. Jacobs. What class do you have second period, Audrey?"

"Math. Mr. Martin."

I made an X where his classroom would be. "OK, that's basically smack in the middle. Here's what we do. We're gonna do a basic force."

"Like a magician," Conor explained. "They tell you to pick any card, but they secretly force you to pick the one they want you to pick."

"Average person needs at least twenty, thirty seconds to get their stuff ready before they're out the door. Audrey, you make sure you're ready to go as soon as the bell rings and hoof it to her classroom. Be there as soon as she walks out. You shouldn't have any problem getting there if you leave right away. Say you want to talk about the show or some homework or whatever. Then, you hold up your water bottle to take a drink, and you realize that it's almost empty. You have to go to the water fountain." I circled the spot where the nearest water fountain was. "But the east side water fountain is already going to be occupied by Conor, who will have slipped out early on a hall pass to the library. The next closest fountain will be this one here, conveniently next to my locker, where Tyler will be after helping me carry my books because he still thinks he owes me for our group project. It will seem totally natural and she'll be in the perfect position to—" As I looked up to finish my sentence, I saw that Audrey was looking at me, wide-eyed. "What?"

"Nothing. Just . . . this really isn't your first rodeo, is it?"

Conor snorted. "First rodeo? Please, they *named* the rodeo after him."

I jabbed him hard with my elbow. "I'm just good at planning things." I shot him a look that said, *Like your funeral if you don't shut up.* He snapped his mouth shut, and I tried to get back into the rhythm of game planning. "So, uh, so yeah. That's basically it for that. Do you think you can handle it?"

Audrey nodded. "I have to talk to her about rehearsal

anyway. It won't be weird for me to be waiting for her when class is over."

"Great. If we can plant the seed in her head in the morning, by rehearsal after school we should have the ball rolling. Then, all we have to do is get invited."

"If you put the idea in her head, I should be able to get you guys invites," Audrey said. "Like I said, we're not super close, but we're close enough."

Usually, I'd be a little more micromanagey on a crew member's first job, but I didn't want to spook her. Besides, if she couldn't handle this on her own, we were doomed right out of the gate.

"That just leaves you, Conor," I said, turning to him. "I want you to get online and find as much footage of the Starcade as you can. From their website. Commercials. YouTube videos from birthday parties. Anything you can find. We need to know what the layout is. What the security is like. Where a person can hide in a pinch."

"Recon and relay," he said, giving a mock salute. "Aye, aye, Captain."

I rolled my eyes at him, but I didn't complain. All his joking aside, Conor was the best set of Fingers I'd ever worked with. If there was info for him to find, he'd find it. The only thing he did better was get in trouble.

The next day, our force went off without a hitch. Tyler, nice guy that he is, had no problem helping me carry my stack of textbooks to my locker, and he had no questions about why I was lugging around every textbook I owned at the same time. It was easy to slip into a conversation about the new VR batting simulator at the downtown Starcade.

"No way, they have VR there now?" he said as he helped me slide books into my locker.

"Yeah, at the Mega Starcade across town," I said for the benefit of Hailey, who'd just walked up with Audrey. Hailey, like most girls at our school, noticed Tyler immediately and started eavesdropping on the conversation, even though I could tell she was trying to be subtle.

"Oh man," he said as he stacked the last book. "I would love to go there. I bet I could rack up so many tickets. But I never get to go."

"Maybe for your birthday?" I suggested casually.

"Maybe," he agreed, completely oblivious to the glint in Hailey's eyes as the wheels in her head started to turn, even if she didn't realize it yet.

As Tyler rushed to his next class, I gave Audrey a quick thumbs-up before rushing off myself.

When I heard two girls arguing about whose version of gossip was accurate—had Hailey canceled horseback riding in Montana or sunbathing in Puerto Rico for a party at the downtown Starcade?—I knew she'd taken the bait. That just left one question: Were we in?

I got my answer when I walked into rehearsal after school.

"Oh, there he is," I heard Hailey say from across the room before she called, "Flounder!" at me. It wasn't that she didn't know my name. At least, I was pretty sure she knew my name. But, apparently, calling castmates by their character names was a theater kid thing. That's what Audrey had said anyway. Hailey was surrounded by the six girls who would play her sisters onstage, including

Audrey, who were all buzzing with excitement, like I'd just missed some spicy news.

"What's up, Ariel?" I said, walking up to her.

"You're friends with Tyler, right?"

"We're chill," I answered, letting her draw her own conclusions without having to say something that I might have to explain to Tyler later.

"Then you should for sure be invited," she said.

"To what?" I said, as if I didn't already know where this was going. You had to go through the motions with these things or else they started to look suspicious. Free piece of advice: Nothing pays more than developing a good poker face early in life.

"My birthday party, duh. I was supposed to go to New York, but I changed my mind. We're doing a party at the Mega Starcade across town instead. Mom said they were all booked up, but she called her guy and then her guy called his guy. You know how it is," she said casually, as if we all had parents who had "guys" they could call to magically make things happen.

I perked up. "Oh, we were just talking about that today. Me and Tyler, I mean." OK, now I was laying it on a bit thick, but Hailey was the linchpin of this plan. If she backed out, we had nothing. We had to make sure she thought she was making a fantastic decision.

When I mentioned Tyler's name, the girls surrounding Hailey gave each other little looks and eyebrow raises, which confirmed my suspicion about having just missed a spicy conversation. She elbowed, not at all discreetly, in their general direction, as she said, "Oh, were you?"

"Yeah, what a coincidence. He said he'd love to try out their VR simulator. He's gonna love this! I mean, he will if you're inviting him. Are you?"

"Yes! I mean, yes, yeah, if he wants to go—I mean, you said he wants to go, right? Right. So I'll invite him. If you think it's a good idea. Do you think it's a good idea? Has he mentioned me at all? Wait, don't tell me."

I could barely keep up with her. If she was that emotional onstage, she was going to bring down the house as Ariel. "You should invite him. He'd like that."

When I said that, Hailey gave a full catnip smile—eyes closed, relaxed, and totally blissed out, like a cat after a big dose of catnip. And, in my experience, blissed-out people tend to be pretty open to suggestion.

"Hey, you know who else you should invite? Conor."

The smile didn't fall off her face, but she looked confused. "Conor? Who's that?"

"There aren't any Conors in our grade," said one of the older mer-girls.

"He's new," I said. "One of my friends from—"

"A new kid? I don't know. I'm only allowed to invite fifty kids."

"Only" fifty? What did she mean "only" fifty? I'd never had that many kids at a party in my—focus! I was losing her.

"I really think that—"

Suddenly, Audrey put up a hand. "It's OK, DJ. You don't have to cover for me."

Huh? "What—"

She cut me off again and moved in front of me just

enough to box me out of the conversation so Hailey's attention would shift to her. "It's embarrassing," she continued, starting to play with her hair. "But the only reason DJ wants you to invite Conor to the party is because . . ." She paused to dip her head down, took a deep breath, and then said all at once, "He knows I have a crush on him."

I think I should repeat my earlier advice about poker faces and their usefulness right about now.

Because when she said that, my entire brain did a spit take but my face didn't change at all. Jumpy insides, calm outsides.

"Oh my gosh, you have a crush on Conor? Also, who's Conor?"

"It's nothing; it's stupid."

"Shut up! Tell me!" Hailey had done a full one-eighty from chill cat to pure gossip bloodhound. And Audrey was playing it perfectly. Shy smile, flustered gestures, she even had a pink blush going on. If I didn't know better—

Wait, *did* I know better?

I mean, she was our Face, sure, but the shortest distance

between two points is a straight line. There was no reason to convince Hailey with a lie when she could just as easily do it with a non-incriminating truth. And, not to repeat myself, she was playing it *perfectly*. Including the little things people don't even notice they're doing when they're nervous, like flicking their eyes around and repeating themselves. And crying on cue was one thing, but blushing? Not even our Face at Grover could do that, and he was a career scammer with a rap sheet so long it would wrap around the school twice—or at least it would if he'd ever been caught. Was this what she'd been planning to do to get Conor in the whole time? Was this why she'd been so confident? Was she going to—

"I guess he's kinda cute, in a dorky way," Hailey was saying when I snapped out of it. Audrey was showing her a pic of Conor she had on her phone. (Why did she have a pic of him on her phone?)

"You don't have to invite him," Audrey said, "but it would be nice to get to hang out with him. We don't have any classes together."

It was the perfect soft sell. Hailey's eyes went gleefully conspiratorial almost instantly. "Oh, don't worry. I got you, girl."

Before she could say anything else, Ms. Andrews, the drama teacher, called us over to get ready. I caught Audrey's arm so she'd hang back with me.

"How'd I do?" she whispered. "I came up with the crush thing on the fly, but I think she really bought it."

"So you *were* faking."

She looked confused for a second and then a wide grin spread across her face. "Oh my gosh, you couldn't tell? You knew what I was doing and you still couldn't tell? I must have been amazing."

"Amazing," I repeated. "Exceeds all expectations."

"OK, now you sound like a report card."

"If I was, that would have been an A plus." She smiled again, but by then, Ms. Andrews had started talking and we had to pay attention.

Or at least look like we were paying attention. I wasn't. I was thinking about Audrey. She was such a good actress, and she was taking to being Face well. Maybe too well?

I shook my head. I was projecting. She wasn't me. Besides, it was just the one job to get Conor off the hook. After that, we'd all be legit again and this would just be a blip on her radar. A funny memory to think about to calm her nerves before she went onstage and killed it.

Chapter Eleven
THE INSIDE MAN

After practice, we swung by Conor's place to see how his R&R was going.

"Not bad," he said, spinning around in his desk chair to face us. "Everyone films everything now. I have a lot of footage, but there are still some blind spots. There are lots of videos of the party area. I have all angles on that. That's in the back right corner. There's a crawl-through sky tunnel system in the front right ceiling that has some good lookout points. Would probably make a good hiding spot too. And then the prize counter is in the middle, toward the back, near the bathrooms. I think the entrance to the employee backroom is in the same hallway with the bathrooms, but I can't be sure.

There's not a lot of good video of that. Here, I have a working map."

He handed us a sketchy map that basically showed us what he'd already told us, with a little extra information. The Skee-Ball lanes were along the left wall. The party area had a karaoke machine and a dance floor. Those hadn't been there the last time we were there.

"What's the security like?" I asked.

"Not good. For us, I mean. Check it out." He swiveled back around in his chair and clicked until he came to a tab that showed a top-down, GPS view of the Starcade. "See? This is the Starcade. This is the bakery next to it. They share an alley, and that's where their dumpsters are. But look." He tapped a spot on the screen. "There's a fence. And that looks like barbed wire."

"Can't hop it," I said, finishing his thought for him.

"Right. And, at our Starcade, there aren't that many employees on the floor at any one time. Two, tops. Real easy to dodge. But look at this video." He switched to a YouTube video titled "Kayla's 8th Birthday Party." The date was a couple of months ago. "Employees are in the red and blue polo shirts."

In the video, the dad filming said, "We're here! Look at all of this." As he swept his camera across the game room floor, I clocked four employees right off the bat. Two in red shirts, walking the floor, one in a blue shirt, working on a machine, and one in blue, mopping up.

He left the video running as he went on. "And there are probably more in the back and in the party area. Now, just because there's a lot of coverage doesn't mean they're all bringing their A game. I mean, a lot of these guys look like they're in high school. But—"

"Wait," I said, pointing at the screen. "Did you see that?"

"See what?" said Audrey.

"Go back. Ten seconds." He did and I stared at the bottom right corner of the screen as the dad moved the camera until, "There! Stop!" He did. I pointed out the spot where I'd been looking. "That kid. I know that kid."

Conor squinted at him. "I don't. Who is he?"

"Oh, wait," Audrey said. "I've seen him around school. Big kid. Really quiet. I think he's a sixth grader."

"*He's* in sixth grade?" Conor yelped. "Jeez, what do his parents feed him? He's massive!"

I checked the date again. It would have been a Wednesday night. What kid was randomly at Mega Starcade on a Wednesday night? He could have been there for a birthday party, but I'd never seen him hanging out with anyone at school. He struck me as kind of a loner.

"Do you know what his name is?" I asked Audrey.

"No. I only see him around. And I've never heard anyone say his name. Actually, I've never heard anyone talk to him at all."

"Yeah, that's what I was . . . wait." That wasn't 100 percent true. I had seen him talking to someone. "I have to make a call."

Most kids my age don't like making phone calls. Texting is easier. But texting leaves a trail. I dialed quickly and waited for someone to pick up.

"Tween Help Hotline. How can I—"

"Oh good, David. It's you."

"DJ?" He sounded confused. Made sense since I never called the helpline, even though he constantly encouraged me to. "You're actually calling—I mean, you're calling! That's great. Wait, I have a script. Let me start over. This is the Tween Help Hotline and I'm here to listen. Anything we talk about might be reported to a member of the Ella Fitzgerald Middle School Counseling Faculty. What's on your mind?"

"I need a name."

"Huh?"

"A name. Of a kid I saw going into the peer counseling office—hey!" He was groaning on his end of the phone. "Don't groan at me!"

"I thought you wanted help!"

"I do want help! Help finding out who this kid is."

"I always tell you. I can't tell you about what happens in my other sessions. I have a responsibility to my clients."

"You have the responsibility not to tell me what happens during the sessions. I'm not asking you for his private business. I just need to know what his name is. That's not confidential."

"It's confidential adjacent."

"We're not playing horseshoes. Adjacent doesn't count." He didn't say anything on the other end, but I could tell he was annoyed. "Come on, David. It's just his name. I could literally walk up to him on Monday and ask him. I'm just asking you now because it's faster."

He sighed. "I . . . I guess it's OK. But just a name. Anything else and—"

"I got it. I won't ask for anything else."

"OK, fine. Who is it?"

"Really big kid. Maybe in sixth grade. Dark hair. Kind of mean-looking. I've never seen him hanging out with anyone. I saw him in the peer counseling room the other day. Oh, and he wears a military-looking jacket."

"That sounds like Monty. Er, Montgomery LaCroix."

"Monty LaCroix," I said, so Audrey and Conor could hear me. Conor immediately opened a fresh browser and started a social media deep dive. "Thanks, David. You're a lifesaver."

I was about to hang up when he stopped me with a "Wait. Why do you want to know?"

"Just curious."

"What? Come on, DJ. I'm not stupid."

"Oh, so you're allowed to have confidentiality, but I can't?"

"You're not a peer counselor, DJ."

"So it's even more impressive that I care so much about confidentiality." I could hear a sharp intake of breath from his end, so I said, "Listen, it's nothing bad. I promise. I just want to ask him some questions, all right? Nothing weird."

"All right. Bye, DJ." I was about to hang up for a second time when he stopped me with another "Wait!"

I sighed. "What is it now?"

He paused. "I'm trying to think of a way to say this that doesn't break confidentiality. Don't . . . mess with him, OK? It wouldn't be good."

Yeah, like I'd been planning on messing with the sixth grader the size of an adult who wore a military jacket and had maybe been expelled from his last school (in Russia) for fighting a teacher, and winning. "Don't worry, I won't. Later."

"Bye."

By the time I hung up, Conor was already talking. "I'm not turning up anything for a Monty LaCroix. Not a super-common first or last name, so you'd think it would be easy to find if it was there. Oh, hold on." He stopped scrolling and tapped the screen. "Felix LaCroix. And we have a friend in common. My older sister! Oh, I bet that's his brother. If he had an older brother, he'd go to the same high school as my sister. Let's check out his profile."

There was only so much of his profile we could see since he and Conor weren't actually friends, but we could see his basic info. School: Acadia High. Birthday: March thirteenth. Workplace—

"Jackpot!" Conor said, eyes lighting up. "It says he works at Starcade! I bet he works at that Starcade!"

"That would explain why Monty was there in the middle of the week. Felix probably got out of class, picked him up, then went to work an evening shift."

This was even better than I'd hoped. If Monty's brother worked at the Starcade, he would have access to inside information. Employees. Schedules. He might even know how the back rooms were set up! We could—

I stopped myself. I'd literally just promised David that all we were going to do was ask him a few questions. That was it.

I clapped Conor on the back. "That's great. This is great. We'll set up a meeting, I'll talk to him, and—"

"Wait, shouldn't Audrey do that?" Conor said, jabbing a thumb at her. "I mean, she's our Face. Sweet-talking and recruiting should be her job, right?"

"Yeah," said Audrey. "I can do that. You said I did a good job with Hailey, right?" She threw a glance at Conor. "Oh, by the way, Hailey thinks I have a crush on you now, so be cool."

"Excuse me?"

"No, no. I should do it. Not that you didn't do a good job. You did. I mean, you did a great job. You know that, you were there." Ugh, I sounded like her impression of a

143

crushing idiot, except I wasn't acting at all. I had to snap out of it. "Just, uh, don't worry about it. I have it covered. All part of the plan."

"Oh, OK. So, what should I do in the meantime?"

"Nothing, nothing. Just relax. Have a good weekend. Chillax."

"CHILLAX?" Conor mouthed incredulously, just out of Audrey's line of sight. He was right. I wanted to die.

Audrey didn't seem to notice though. "All right. Well, if you don't need me, I should go home. But you will call me if you do, right? You have my number."

"Of course, yeah."

Conor rolled his eyes at me. "Come on, Auds. I'll show you out."

They disappeared for about a minute and then I heard the front door slam. When Conor came back in, his hands were thrown up and he had the biggest, *Dude, really?* look on his face.

"I know," I said, burying my head in my hands.

"What was that?"

"I know."

"What happened to 'jumpy insides, calm outsides'? That was jumpy insides, jumpier outsides. I mean, 'chillax'? Who are you?"

"*I know.* I was there for all of that, Conor. Trust me, I know."

"I'm serious," he said as he dropped back into his chair. "I was worried about Audrey since she's brand-new and squeaky clean, but now I'm more worried about you. She can work with us. Can you?"

"I'm fine," I said unconvincingly, even to myself. Before he could call me on it, I said, "Bethany is here, right?"

"I didn't check, but her car is in the driveway. She's probably in her room."

"Good. We should ask her about Felix and Monty now. The party's on Wednesday. If we leave it to Monday, we won't have a lot of wiggle room to plan. And if he won't talk to us, that's two days down the drain."

"OK, what do we tell her?"

"The truth," I said. "Just not why we want it. Come on."

We went down the hall and knocked on Bethany's door. Bethany was Conor's other sister. She was in tenth grade, and she'd babysat for me since she was twelve. Conor complained about her a lot, but I always thought she was fun. Of course, I didn't actually have to live with her.

After a few seconds, she opened the door and glanced at us with mismatched red and brown eyes. "Oh, what's up, DJ? I didn't know you were here." When she smiled, I saw a flash of vampire fangs.

"Those look really good," I said, pointing at her teeth.

"You think so? How about my voice? I've been practicing talking around them since I got them. I don't wanna lisp. The vampires in *Buffy* were always lisping. And, like, what's the point of going all out with the nice contacts and the custom cape if I sound like Daffy Duck the entire time?"

"You sound good," I assured her. "The people at the fantasy convention tomorrow are gonna be impressed."

"Aww, thanks, DJ." She started closing the door and

then stopped. "Oh, wait. You didn't come in here to talk about my cosplay. What did you guys want?"

"Do you know a kid named Felix LaCroix?" Conor asked.

"Yeah," she said. "He's in my AP Bio class. He's pretty smart, but he argues with the teacher a lot. Kind of a punk. Why?"

"Does he ever talk about his brother?" I asked.

"Um, I don't know. We're not really friends. I didn't even know he had a brother. Wait, no. He did mention he had a little brother when we were doing Punnett squares."

Conor and I exchanged a quick look. More confirmation that we had the right kid. "Do you have his number?" I asked. "We need to ask his little brother about a project, but he's not on social media."

"A project?" she said with an eyebrow raised. No one knew the extent of all the jobs I'd pulled off with Conor and our various crews, but Bethany wasn't dumb. She knew a lot.

"It's something for school," I said. Which was true. It

wasn't school sanctioned, but it definitely had to do with school.

Like I said, Bethany wasn't dumb, but she also didn't care about standing in our way most of the time. "Yeah, hold on. I'll text it to you." She pulled out her phone and fiddled with it for a few seconds. Conor's phone pinged from his pocket. "There you go. Anything else?"

"That's it. Thanks, Bethany."

"Yeah, thanks, Beth."

"Later, dudes."

She went back to her room to finish her vampire costume, and we went back to Conor's room to make a call.

"Are you sure you don't want Audrey to handle this?" Conor said as I dialed.

"I'll be fine. I recruited her, didn't I?"

Of course, I thought as the phone began to ring, *she was a nice girl I was doing the show with who I'd low-key wanted to talk to for months and he was a giant of a kid who maybe beat up a teacher*. On second thought, maybe Audrey should be the one to—

"Hello?" It was an annoyed-sounding teenage boy. "This better not be another spam call or I swear—"

"No, no, no. I'm DJ. Bethany's brother's friend. I go to school with your brother, Monty."

There was a long pause. "What do you want with Monty? You got trouble with him?"

"No!" I said, trying to steer the conversation from the immediately drastic turn it was taking. If Monty was so quick to fight that that's how his brother screened his calls, I needed to redirect this conversion pronto. What did he do? What did he like? I thought about the last time I'd seen him, and an idea hit me. "Listen, I've been going to peer counseling sessions and my guy gave me this pamphlet. I usually don't really read them, but I did this time and it said that it's good to reach out to new people." I wanted to hug David for forcing me to read that stupid pamphlet. "I was going to message Monty online, but I couldn't find him. Is he there? Can you ask him if he wants to, you know, hang out?"

Another long pause. "What did you say your name was again?"

"DJ. I'm in seventh grade."

"One second." There was some rustling on the other side of the phone and then some talking I couldn't make out.

"How's it going?" Conor mouthed. I made a fifty-fifty tilting gesture with my hand. I covered the receiver to say that I wasn't really sure, when Felix came back on.

"OK, yeah. What time?"

I shot Conor a thumbs-up. "Uh, noon tomorrow? At the Starcade?"

"Ugh. OK, fine. Tomorrow at the Starcade. But you better not be late."

"Yeah, no prob—" Click. The line went dead. "OK, his brother isn't the best go-between in the world, but we have our meeting."

"I heard. So, what? We scrounge up a couple of tokens, play some Skee-Ball, pump him for info, and then cut him loose?"

"Yeah. We should also bring some tickets to sweeten the pot if we have to. Not enough that he's suspicious of where we got them, but enough to make him want to talk if he's stubborn. And, based on that conversation with his brother, I feel like he might be."

"Gotcha. You want me there as backup?"

"Of course."

"And Audrey?"

"Does not need to be there." He gave me a hard look. "What?"

"Come on, DJ. If she's our Face, she's gotta be our Face. What was the point of bringing her in if you're gonna coddle her? You always say, if we're gonna be a team, there's gotta be trust. Is she on the team or not?"

"There's no team," I said. "We don't need to drag her into every little detail of this. This is a one-time thing and then we're done."

"Whatever you say, boss," he said in the way that he does when he's mentally dunking whatever I just said into the trash.

I frowned but didn't say anything.

The next day, Conor and I were at Starcade at twelve

sharp. Actually, we were there at eleven thirty because I didn't want to know what would happen if we were late. Monty was early too, which wasn't surprising. Arriving early was a power move. Arriving late was also a power move depending on the situation, but it didn't matter. We were both there.

Conor noticed him coming out of the black pickup truck first.

He thumped me on the back and said, "Look. There he is."

I watched him climb out of the truck, trademark army jacket on even though it really wasn't that cold outside. His brother was in the driver's seat—long, stringy blond hair tied into a bun. "I'll be in the parking lot," he yelled over the rock music that was pouring out of his speakers. "Text me when you're ready to leave." Monty waved at him before turning toward us.

"Of course it had to be the scariest dude at school," Conor muttered under his breath as Monty approached us.

I waved Monty over and elbowed Conor at the same

time. "Shut up. He'll hear you." He was almost for sure out of earshot, but we were on a mission. I didn't need Conor running his mouth. I ran through my strategy in my head one more time. Skee-Ball. Talk about school. Talk about Starcade. Segue into his trip to the downtown Starcade. We only had a few tokens, so we didn't have a lot of time to hold his attention. This had to be quick and clean.

He stopped in front of us and, man, I really couldn't believe this kid was only in sixth grade. He was almost as tall as my dad, and broad, but in a buff way. Not just baby fat. My entire being did one of those huge, cartoon-style gulps, but I didn't let it show.

"Hey, Monty," I said. "I don't think we've actually talked before. I'm DJ. That's my friend Conor. I was gonna mention he was coming before your brother hung up on me."

"Hi," he said in the smallest voice. If I hadn't been looking at him, I wouldn't have guessed he was the one who'd talked. It was like a mouse had possessed a gorilla. And he wasn't quite making eye contact either. He was mainly looking at his shoes. "Thanks for inviting me. I still don't really know that many people here."

Conor and I looked at each other out of the corners of our eyes. Curveball, but he didn't need to know that.

"Yeah, of course. I've seen you around school, but we never really got the chance to talk. Sorry we don't have that many tokens though. We don't get our allowances until next week."

"Oh, that's OK. My brother used to work at a Starcade and he got this for me." He pulled a certificate out of his pocket. It was a coupon for fifty free tokens. "I was saving it for something special, and then you called so I thought it was a good time to use it."

"Uh, it's the *perfect* time to use it," Conor said. Yeah, right while we were using him. "Lead the way, my man."

Chapter Twelve
COMING CLEAN

"I can't believe it," Conor whispered as we watched Monty cash in his certificate for tokens. "He's a total pushover. This is great!"

"Mm-hm." His shy smile as he'd opened the door for us was playing in my head on a loop. He was genuinely excited to be making friends. I didn't need to be a Face to read that.

"DJ? Yo, are you paying attention?"

"Huh?"

"Dude, get your head in the game. He's coming back."

"What? Oh, yeah, right." I had to pull it together.

He came over with the fifty tokens divided among three little cups. "Here," he said, holding two of them out.

"There were two extra but I put them in these cups so you guys could have them."

I could feel my karma levels dropping into negative numbers.

Conor clearly wasn't having the same problem as me because he yanked away the cup he was offered and said, "Awesome! Let's play Skee-Ball!"

"So," Conor said as he slotted a token into his Skee-Ball machine. "I heard you're new."

"Yeah. My whole family moved from Canada because my mom got a job at the medical supply company in town."

"Oh my gosh, Canada!" Conor mouthed when Monty glanced away from us to put in his own token. I quickly put a finger to my lips and then turned it to a nose scratch when Monty popped back up.

"Canada. Interesting. How do you like it here so far?"

He shrugged. "It's OK. Kinda lonely." He tugged nervously on his left jacket sleeve. "But it's been fine. No one messes with me, so that's good at least. And, now that you guys are hanging out with me, maybe I'll start making friends."

"I need to use the bathroom," I said, setting down my cup of tokens and turning abruptly. I wasn't even walking toward the bathroom; I was just walking away, like I could walk away from my guilt. Nope, it followed me, and so did Conor.

"Yo," he said, grabbing my shoulder once we were hidden by a row of arcade cabinets. "What are you doing? You're blowing it!"

"I can't do it."

"Do what? Play Skee-Ball and ask him some questions?"

"Manipulate him!"

"You manipulated Hailey," he pointed out.

"That's different."

"How?"

"There was nothing behind that. She wouldn't really care if she found out we were using her. But you saw him. He wants to make real friends!"

"So? Let's play with him for a little bit. Make his day. Then get back to the job."

"I can't do this, Conor."

He threw up his hands. "I knew it! This is about our last job, isn't it?! You think it's gonna turn out the same way but news flash! Monty isn't—"

"Were you guys talking about me?"

For such a big dude, Monty was stealthy. Or maybe it was the combo of the loud arcade and our heated conversation. Either way, boom. There he was.

Conor and I shot each other a glance.

"No," he said at the same time I said, "Yes."

Monty's shoulders dropped. "Oh. I get it." He sighed and pulled out his phone, I guessed to call his brother.

"No, no, no. Wait." I put up my hands, full surrender. "We were talking about you, but not the way you think. We weren't playing a prank on you or anything. We just—" Guilty conscience or not, I didn't want to be talking about sensitive information out in the open, especially since we'd already gotten caught once in the past five minutes. "Here," I said, motioning for him to duck into an empty photo booth with us. It was a tight squeeze, but we made it work.

"OK," I said, once the curtain was closed. "Here's the deal. We think you have some info we could use and we thought you were kind of a bad kid so we were going to bribe you with some tickets and ask you, but then you showed up and you were nice and you gave us your extra tokens—I mean, who does that? So I felt bad about taking advantage of you and when you heard us talking, I was saying we should call it off. We weren't trying to pick on you. I didn't want you to feel bad. I'm sorry. And, for the record, I really do go to peer counseling with David."

Let me tell you, you don't know the meaning of an awkward silence until you've had an awkward silence while standing nose to armpit inside a photo booth that was not made to hold three people.

After what felt like forever, Monty finally said, "What did you want to know?"

"About the Mega Starcade downtown. The setup. The people working there. Stuff like that."

Another giant silence in the middle of the ear-shatteringly loud arcade.

"That's it?"

"Yeah. Like I said, I'm sor—"

"I thought you were going to say something bad."

"Uh . . . what?"

The tension in his body basically melted away. It actually made it harder to fit in the booth now that he wasn't all hunched over. "I got picked on all the time at my old school so Felix said I should talk less and act tough so no one would mess with me. So it's not your fault you thought I was mean."

"See?" Conor said. "It's no big deal. I told you he'd be cool."

"Just because he's saying it now doesn't mean it would be cool to do without asking."

"Fine, we'll ask him. Monty, will you tell us about the downtown Starcade?"

"Sure."

Conor held up a hand to him like he was saying, *See?*

"Why do you want to know about the Starcade though?" Monty asked.

"For something we're doing," Conor said. "Kind of a group project."

"Can I help?"

Conor and I shot each other another glance.

"Yes," he said at the same time I said, "No."

"Come on!" Conor hissed. "You said we needed a full crew, right? Well, here's the Muscle."

"No. He wants to hang out, not do a *group project*. You don't make friends during *group projects*."

"We became friends during a *group project*."

"Why do you two keep saying *group project* like that?" Monty asked.

"Like what?" Conor said, right before a hand yanked back the photo booth curtain.

"There you guys are," Audrey said. "I've been looking all over for you."

"Audrey?" I croaked. "What are you doing here?"

"Conor texted me," she said. "Next time, say photo booth. I thought you meant booth like a table."

"My bad," he said. "And false alarm. We're back on track. Oh, and meet Monty. Last member of our crew."

"Oh!" she said brightly. "Nice to meet you. I'm Audrey."

"What? No!" I cried.

"No, my name isn't Audrey?"

"No, I mean no Monty's not working on the *group project.*"

Audrey turned to Conor. "Is that what we're calling it now?"

"Nah. He's just being weird about Monty, but don't worry. He's gonna be our Muscle."

"No!" I had to stop this before it got out of control. I was the Brains. It was my job. "He is not going to be our Muscle. And, honestly, Audrey, you shouldn't be our Face."

"What?"

"I'm not saying you didn't do a good job setting up the party and getting us invites, but—"

"No, it's been good! I've actually been really excited about it. And, after I left yesterday, I listened to a bunch of musical soundtracks about con men. *The Music Man. Dirty Rotten Scoundrels. Catch Me if You Can.* You know, to get into character."

"That's exactly why you shouldn't be our Face! Is that really the kind of character you want to be getting into?"

She flinched back from me before taking a defensive stance. "Well *you* do it."

"Yeah, I do. Which is why you should listen to me when I say you *shouldn't* do it."

She stared at me for a couple of seconds before breaking eye contact and looking at Conor. "Something happened, didn't it? At your old school, before you started at Fitz."

"Yes," he said at the same time I said, "No." That was zero for three. We were really off our rhythm today.

I sighed. "OK, yes, something happened." When she looked at me expectantly, I said, "Can we at least sit down? I can't breathe in here."

She held the curtain open for us and we made our way to one of the eating booths. I did a quick scan to make sure no one was eavesdropping before I said, "At our old school, we were pretty notorious."

"For hustles," Conor added for Monty, helpfully.

"I was going to phrase it differently, but sure. Hustles, cons, jobs, whatever. We were a one-stop shop. We could get basically anything done. We got schedules moved around. We got weekend detentions canceled. We rigged an election once."

"Wow."

"It was just for the sixth-grade rep."

"Still."

"Anyway, near the end of the year, we got a big job. This one teacher had a policy where, if she lost a student's test, they would automatically get an A. Someone really needed that A, and they were willing to pay a lot of holos if we made sure she lost that test."

"Holos are what we used instead of tickets at Grover," Conor chimed in. "I think they're way cooler than tickets, but when in Rome—" I glared at him. "OK, shutting up."

"*Anyway,* it was a complicated plan and I won't get into all the details, but a key part of the plan was that we needed a distraction during a certain art class during fourth period. I did some digging and I found out that Mr. Danvers—that was the art teacher—was really scared of spiders. So I think, OK. That's easy enough to work with. I catch this huge spider in my backyard and I look it up to make sure it's not venomous enough to actually hurt anyone. Then, I had a casual conversation with him where I steered the conversation to spiders to make sure he wasn't allergic to them or anything. He wasn't. So I think it's all good to go."

"And then it went wrong?" she guessed.

I shook my head. "It went right. Way too right. I thought Mr. Danvers was just scared of spiders, you know, like a normal person is scared of something. He wasn't just scared of spiders. He was full-on arachnophobic. I found out later that he fell into a nest of spiders when he was, like, seven. It messed him up for life. I went in there pretending like I was delivering something from the library and I snuck the spider onto his sleeve." I shuddered, remembering the scene. "It was awful. He knocked over so much paint. He ruined, like, an entire periods' projects. And then he just, like, shut down. Like he wasn't even a person. There was nothing going on behind his eyes. The nurse had to literally drag him out of the classroom, and then he was off for two weeks. It was one of our most successful jobs ever, but, after watching that, I felt sick."

"He didn't take any more jobs after that," Conor said. "And, at the end of the year, he got his parents to transfer him to the Fitz. I told him he was being crazy, but—"

"I needed a fresh start," I said. "They weren't able to pin it on me, but I think a couple of admins were suspicious. Besides, I like it too much. The planning, the figuring things out, the little victories. It's so great. But that is the worst thing I've ever done to someone, and it happened because I just had to do a stupid job. So when I look at you, and *you* tell me, 'I want to help with this group project' and you tell me, 'Oh, I really like getting into character,' it makes *me* feel like I'm being a terrible person and dragging you down with me."

"Oh, DJ." Audrey reached across the table, stretched out her hand, and flicked me square in the middle of the forehead.

"Ow! What was that for?"

"That's why you didn't want to let me help you yesterday? I thought it was going to be something bad."

"Why do people keep saying that to me today?"

"I mean, don't get me wrong. That wasn't good, what you did. You shouldn't have done it. You definitely went too far. But, you're not, like, evil. You made sure the spider wasn't venomous and you made sure the guy wasn't allergic. I bet a lot of people wouldn't have even thought to check, or they wouldn't have cared enough. And you felt bad enough that you changed schools, even though you didn't get caught. And clearly, you're still beating yourself up over it, so your conscience isn't broken. Plus, the only reason you're doing this job in the first place is to help Conor. So, suck it up, and let me help you! And

Monty, if he wants to. I don't really know what his deal is."

Before I could work out a response, Conor snorted. "I can't believe I didn't want to recruit you. You're awesome."

She shushed him before saying, "If you wanna talk about it more, we can, but I promise you, I'm not going to do this one job and then turn to a life of crime or whatever you think is going to happen. I just want to help you guys, OK?"

I took a deep breath and made eye contact with Audrey, Monty, and then Conor. "OK. But we have to do it without any innocent bystanders getting hurt, all right? No permanent damage. Like that thing they say about hiking. Leave nothing but footprints, take nothing but pictures. And all the tickets we're gonna be taking, obviously."

"Is that what you guys are doing?" Monty asked.

"Yeah, but just the ones they throw away," Audrey explained.

"Don't they shred those?"

Conor put a hand on his shoulder. "Buddy, we need to get you caught up."

"Let's go to my place," Audrey suggested.

So we did. We explained the situation so far to Monty, and he filled in the blanks in Conor's map of the Mega Starcade.

"My brother used to work there, so I hung out there a lot."

"Used to?" I asked.

"Yeah, he was five minutes late one day because he stopped to check on a lady who was in a car crash, and the manager fired him."

"Gonna be honest," said Audrey. "Sounds like a terrible job."

"The job was fine. That specific manager just had it out for him. He had it out for everyone, honestly. He was always patrolling the place like it was an army base or something important."

That sounded like it could be a problem. "Do you know if he still works there?"

"I think so."

"Do you know if he'll be working there Wednesday night?"

"My brother still has a few friends who work there. I can have him find out. Hold on, I'll text him." Felix had gone into town, now that he knew his brother was having a good time and wouldn't need to make a speedy escape. He may have been a punk, but he obviously had a soft spot for his little brother.

"OK, great. Conor, how many ticket-counter machines did you see?"

"Ten that I saw. That's double what they have at the local Starcade. There will be more than enough tickets."

"Great. Now all we need to do is figure out a way to get into that alley. We can't hop the fence. And we're not cutting through it with bolt cutters, Conor, so don't even suggest it."

"I wasn't gonna."

"Yes, you were."

"Yes, I was."

"This hallway opens into the break room, which has a door to the alley," Audrey said, pointing it out where Monty had added it to the map. "Can we sneak through there?"

We all turned to Monty, who shook his head. "They're pretty strict about not letting kids back there. I couldn't even go back there when my brother was working, and there's always at least one worker in that area. It would be really hard to get away with it even once. We'd have to get there and back, more than once, carrying huge bags of tickets." But then his face brightened suddenly. "Oh!"

"Oh, what?"

"The Birthday Closet!"

"What?"

"The Birthday Closet," he repeated, circling a spot on the map to the middle of the far right wall. "It's a little storage area out on the floor, near these two ticket counters. The old-style ones. When there's a really busy day, like when they have a bunch of back-to-back birthday parties, and they don't have time to go all the way to the alley, they'll just stuff the bags in this closet since it's close and there's no food in them that will smell bad. I mean, if that's helpful."

"If that's helpful?" I said incredulously. "Uh, yeah,

that's helpful. Oh my gosh, that changes everything. If we can just grab the tickets from there, we don't have to deal with the alley at all. And, if an employee opens the door and a bag is missing, they'll just assume that someone put it in the trash."

Monty's phone pinged. "Oh, it's my brother. He says Tony isn't working Wednesday night. He has the morning shift. Dave has the night shift. He's cooler."

"Great." That was one less thing to worry about. "Also, do you know what the different shirt colors mean? Conor said some of them were wearing red shirts and some were wearing blue shirts."

"One color is for the people on the manager track. I don't remember which though."

"Hey, I have a question," said Conor. "Don't most jobs come with, like, rule books that explain this stuff? Does your brother still have his copy?"

"Oh yeah, they sent him a PDF when he was hired. I bet he still has it in his emails."

"That's great. Guys, this is all great."

Audrey punched me lightly on the shoulder. "And you didn't want us to help you." She smiled, and so did I.

By the time Wednesday rolled around, we were all ready to go, save for one little loose end. Fortunately, she wasn't very hard to track down.

Mariposa didn't have a free period for business like Lucky did, but most mornings, when she wasn't handling something for Lucky, she was posted up in the cafeteria near the corner window. Most kids passed through the cafeteria on their way in, so it was a good way of keeping tabs on who was around. Also, the French toast sticks weren't half bad.

When I walked in, she was at her usual table, with Cami and Drew sitting across from her. Cami and Drew ran the Trading Post, which was one of the more successful business operations at the Fitz. Instead of contraband, they skewed more artsy—beaded bracelets, bookmarks—the inventory changed with the trends. The Trading Post only opened once a week, and to figure out where it was going to be set up, you had to find where they'd stuck a Post-it.

It was like a game. People loved it. They were never in the same place twice in a row and they definitely didn't make personal visits.

Except, apparently, for Mariposa.

Drew had one of those binders people keep trading cards in spread out in front of her, but instead of trading cards, the pockets were filled with their latest piece of inventory: temporary tattoos.

As Drew flipped through the pages of colorful animals, emojis, and backward lettering, Cami spoke to Mariposa apologetically.

"Our inventory is a little low right now. Cheerleading squad cleaned us out of most of the Glitz and Glitter collection yesterday. But we just got some really cool glow-in-the-dark ones. And I don't know how you feel about dragons but—"

She gestured for Drew to flip forward in the binder, but Mariposa put up a hand to stop her when she noticed me walking up. Her eyes flicked from my face to the folder I was holding and then she said, "I have to take an appointment. We'll talk when you're fully stocked. You know what I want."

"Of course," said Cami, getting up with Drew together in one motion and walking away, like they'd practiced it, perfectly in sync.

"I hope you're not here to try to bribe me to get you out of this," Mariposa said as I took the seat across from her. "Because I couldn't even if I wanted to, which I don't."

"No. I didn't come about that."

She raised an eyebrow at me, which was fair.

"OK, it's a little about that, but not in the way that you're thinking."

Lucky was who we were most worried about. He was the one who wanted the tickets. He was the one who was threatening to rocket boost us. But Mariposa had been the one running the tournament. Conor hadn't just crossed Lucky. He'd also crossed her.

"I had a talk with Conor about what he did and we both agree that it was highly disrespectful to not only the operation, but you personally."

Mariposa's shoulders shook slightly the way they do when you laugh, except her deadpan expression didn't change. "Well, that makes three of us. What's your point?"

"Conor was the first to, uh, *test* your system but he won't be the last." I slid the folder I'd brought across the table to her. "This should help with that."

She looked at me dubiously before opening the folder and scanning the sheets of paper inside. "Info on all the hacks Conor used are in there," I explained. "And how to detect them."

"I have a system for that now," she muttered under her breath, not taking her eyes off Conor's notes.

"This is better," I said. "Conor modded it himself. You caught him because he was sloppy, not because his code was bad."

She kept scanning through the notes. They were a little technical, but I'd had Conor write them up so even a non-techy person could follow them. I didn't know how much Mariposa knew about that kind of stuff, but she didn't look confused by anything that was written down, and when she finally spoke again, her question wasn't a technical one.

"Whose idea was this?"

"The mods?"

"The apology."

"What do you think?"

She gave me half a smirk. "I think you're really sticking your neck out for this kid when you don't have to. This isn't your problem. You don't have to do this."

She was right. But she was also so wrong I had to stop a laugh in my throat.

"I kinda do."

"Well, then," she said, leaning back in her chair and looking at me like I was a pet that was about to attempt a trick. "I hope you're feeling lucky."

Chapter Thirteen
KEEP IT SIMPLE

You know how sometimes you go back to a place you used to love and it's just not as good as you remember? Not as big or cool or fun?

The Mega Starcade wasn't like that. The moment I walked in on Wednesday evening, it instantly lived up to my memory and its name. It was mega loud, mega bright, and mega full of screaming kids. If anything, it was even more impressive now. There were more lights, more games, more to do. Of course, I already knew all that from studying footage of the layout with the team, but footage is one thing. Actually being there is another.

As she walked in with me, my mom rubbed her eyes.

"I don't know how you can stand this. It's too dark *and* too bright in here. How is that possible? And the noise." I could tell she wanted to drop me off and leave as quickly as possible, which was exactly what I wanted too. A Starcade party package was exactly two hours long, so we were on a tight schedule.

We'd all met up that morning before school started to run through the plan one last time. It was honestly pretty simple, but all the best plans are.

"OK," I said. "The three of us are getting dropped off by our parents for the party. Monty, you're gonna catch a ride with Conor because his parents won't care." Plan A had been to have Felix drive Monty, but he'd said the only way he'd go back there was if he were dead or if Tony were, so that was a no go.

"Once we're there, we get tons of face time at the party, so people specifically remember us doing normal, non-suspicious party stuff. Then, Audrey, your job is to make distractions so Conor can grab the tickets, one bag at a time, and feed them into the machines. We're going to want to launder as many bags as possible while we're onsite. Even between the four of us, there's only so many tickets we could realistically win in one night. We're going to need around eight bags to be safe, so you'll have to get creative with the distractions."

"I'm always creative," she said with a wink. Conor kicked me under the table. I kicked him back and then cleared my throat before I kept going.

"I think you'll be fine to play it by ear, but just in case, we might want to run through some common distractions with you. Classic Face stuff. You know, the Crybaby, the Horn of Plenty, the Aunt Karen."

"Aunt Karen?" she asked.

I pointed at Conor who, on cue, did a reasonable impression of his aunt's shrill, "I want to speak to your manager!"

"Ah," said Audrey. "Got it."

"And then there's more complicated stuff, like the Duck Lemonade or the Moonwalking Bear, but we're trying to keep things simple, so they shouldn't come into play."

She nudged Monty. "If his face wasn't so serious right now, I'd think he was making up those names to mess with us."

"He's not," Conor confirmed. "And I have the bite mark to prove it."

I stopped him before he could roll up his sleeve and show her. "She doesn't need to see that. That wasn't the Moonwalking Bear, that was you being an idiot and you know it."

"Well, I got rid of all the footage, so I guess we'll never know, will we?"

I rolled my eyes at him and turned to Monty.

"Monty, you already did great with getting us all that inside info, but you're also Muscle for this job. But soft Muscle. You don't actually need to rough anyone up. You just need to be ready to stand somewhere and look tough if I ask you to."

"I'm good at that," he said brightly, completely undermining his tough-guy look.

"I know. That's why you have the job."

"And what are you doing while we're doing all the heavy lifting?" Conor joked, like he didn't already know.

"Keeping an eye on everything, as usual. This is gonna be a dark space filled with screaming kids. Things that we don't expect are going to happen, but that's fine. We just need to stick together and this will go as smoothly as a job like this can. And, if you want to back out, it's not too late to—" This time, Conor and Audrey both flicked me at almost the same time. "OK, message received. I'll stop asking. Oh, and remember the dress code. No bright colors. We don't want to stand out when we're sneaking around."

Only about a minute inside the Starcade, I was already starting to sweat a little in my gray hoodie, but it was fine. Two hours wasn't a long time.

Mom walked me up to the check-in desk, where there was already a small line of kids and their parents. Some of them I recognized from school. They were all holding wrapped boxes or gift bags in their hands, and as they approached the counter, an employee wearing a red polo shirt would ask them a couple of questions and then put a little green wristband around the kid's wrist. Most of the kids also got a stamp on the back of their right hand, and so did the adult they were with—but not all of them. Once they were done getting checked in, some of the adults went toward the party area with their kids. Some made a hard U-turn for the exit. I guessed they had the same opinion of the Mega Starcade as my mom.

"Are you here for a party?" the woman behind the counter asked as we got to the front. She was a red shirt. Those were the employees on track to be managers one day, according to the manual Monty had snagged for us. He said that they tended to be a little stricter, unlike the blue shirts, who were usually teenage temps like his brother had been.

"Yeah. Hailey's party."

"Name?"

"Darius James," said my mom. "Or it might be under DJ."

The woman looked at her computer screen for a few seconds before pressing a button and saying, "Will you be staying too?"

"No. I'll be back to pick him up at the end of the party."

"All right. Can I see your hand please?" she asked me. I gave it to her and she wrapped a green, glow-in-the-dark paper wristband around my wrist. It was my ticket in and out of the reserved party area. As she adjusted the wristband she asked, "How old are you, DJ?"

"Twelve," I answered truthfully because my mom was standing behind me. Thirteen is the answer I wanted to give. The Mega Starcade had more security measures than the local one. Anyone over thirteen could go in and out whenever they felt like it, but if you were twelve and under, you needed to be released to a parent or guardian with a matching stamp. It tied me down a little, but not much more than the wristband. With it, they wouldn't let me out until the party was over. Besides, if I really needed to get out for some reason, I was sure I could count on Audrey to give me some cover.

The red shirt pressed a stamp on the back of my hand. At first, it didn't show, but I knew it was made from a special ink that would only appear under UV lights and wouldn't fade for at least twelve hours, even with soap or alcohol pads. Sure enough, when she shone a UV penlight on it to make sure it printed correctly, I saw that it was a shooting star with the number 237 in the center.

She repeated the process with Mom and then said, "You're all set. You can come pick him up in two hours. DJ, you'll be in party area two. That's right over there. Have fun."

"Thanks." Mom turned to me and said, "Call me if you need to leave early," before booking it out of there as quickly as she could.

I took a deep breath. We were on the clock. It was time for step one: mingling. That meant heading over to the party area, just like I was supposed to. So far, so good.

The main dining area of the Starcade was in the top right corner of the room, right in front of the stage. Last time I'd been there, it had been the location of a show involving space cadets and a costumed alien that was almost as cheesy as their pizza. The show was still running, but they'd also added karaoke and a small, light-up dance floor. The private party areas were up a short flight of stairs, overlooking the dining floor and stage.

Hailey was at the entrance to our roped-off area, welcoming her guests and collecting presents. When she saw me, she squealed, "Flounder!"

"Hey, Ariel," I said, handing her the gift bag. "Happy birthday."

"Thanks!" Then, she leaned in and said in a low voice, "And thanks for encouraging me to invite Tyler. I checked the karaoke catalog and there are so many duets. He isn't gonna know what hit him. I don't know if he likes singing in public, but no one says no to the birthday girl."

So I wasn't the only one with a secret, elaborate plan going on tonight. Romance jobs were the one type I never took—too many variables. They were always a total toss-up. But Hailey looked like she had run all those variables and liked what she saw.

"Well, good luck with that. Hey, when can we go out on the game floor?"

"You can go now," she said. "Just pick up a cup of tokens from my mom over there and be back in half an hour for pizza. They'll make an announcement on the loudspeaker."

"Got it. Again, happy birthday."

I went and got my tokens and then headed back down to our rendezvous point. Or, I should say, down and then back up. The multicolored sky tunnels snaked their way across the ceiling of the Starcade and had two cave-like areas at each dead end with a clear, plastic window looking out on the game floor. You could see almost the entire Starcade from between the two of them. The only blind spot was part of the kiddie play area directly below. They were fantastic vantage points. We'd picked the one to the right, overlooking the Birthday Closet, as our home base.

I took off my shoes, put them in a little cubby, and then climbed up.

Conor and Monty were already there. Monty was basically curled into himself, trying to take up as little space as possible, and he still took up more space than Conor or me. On the plus side, him just being there was making kids keep their distance. We had the space to ourselves.

"Have you been waiting long?" I asked.

"Nah," Conor said. "We just got up here a few minutes ago. I've been scoping out the security. I've seen two red shirts and three blue shirts on the floor. And I haven't seen Dave yet."

"He's probably in the back," Monty said. "Felix says they have an Xbox back there they take turns with to cool off."

"If we're lucky, he hits a hot streak and he's back there all night." I was about to say that Audrey had called a few minutes before I'd arrived and said she was close, but I was saved the explanation when I felt a tap on my shoulder.

"Huh? Oh, there you are, Audrey."

"Hey. I got up here as soon as I could. Hailey wanted to gossip."

"You're good. We're right on schedule. We have about half an hour before we need to be back at the party. We should be able to get through at least two bags of tickets by then if we start now. Conor, do you have the mega bags?"

"Yeah, Monty got them from the counter when he came in." He pulled out a few big, clear, trash-type bags with the Starcade logo on them, which were made for hauling around huge amounts of tickets. Most kids didn't make that many in one go, but they kept them around for power gamers. We were going to have to transfer the tickets from the black trash bags to the clear ticket carriers if we didn't want to look suspicious lugging around what was supposed to be garbage. And any we didn't launder, we could bring home in the bags like we'd won them.

"OK, like we said. Grab the bag and bring it to the big stall in the bathroom. Monty can help you swap them out as quickly as possible, or stand guard and scare people off if that's more helpful. Then we'll feed them into the machine. Monty, I'm sending you down with Audrey for now. Some of her distractions are two-man operations, and she won't know which ones to use until she's on the floor."

He nodded. "Got it."

I pulled out my phone. "Everyone got your earbuds?"

They all nodded and pulled them out. The Bluetooth earbuds were from Conor's tech kit. We needed to be able to talk to each other at all times. Audrey could hide hers under her hair, and I could hide mine under my hoodie. Monty and Conor were both wearing beanies to cover theirs. I synced my earbuds to my phone and then started a group call.

"Can you all hear me?" I asked. Thumbs-up from everyone. "OK, great. I'll be up here, watching. Don't all go out at once. Monty, you first. Then Conor. Then Audrey." They all nodded. I took a breath. "Guys—"

"I swear, if you try to call this off again—" Audrey started.

"No. I was just going to say, we got this."

"We got this," Monty repeated, before nodding and crawling back out of the sky tunnels.

When he turned the corner, Conor punched me in the shoulder. "We got this."

Conor exited in the other direction, the one with the slide.

After a few seconds, I saw both of them pop out of opposite ends of the structure and walk past each other like strangers. That just left me and Audrey.

She put her hand on my shoulder and smiled. "Don't worry, DJ. We got this." I could feel blood rushing to my cheeks. I opened my mouth to say—I'm not sure what, but then I remembered we were all mic'd up and anything that I said, Monty and Conor would hear too, even if they weren't with us. So, instead, I just nodded and said, "We got this. Go."

She did and, soon, she was on the floor too. So now it was time for me to do my job. I scanned the game floor. Conor was near the Birthday Closet, playing whack-a-mole and eyeing the closet every few seconds. There was a tall blue shirt next to him, sweeping up something I couldn't quite see. I didn't see any other employees in the vicinity, and there were mostly kiddie games in that area, so the people there were mainly parents occupied by their small kids.

"Con, I don't see any other employees here besides that one tall blue shirt."

"Me either," he said. "But I think he'll be here for a while. You probably can't see it from up there but there's a giant popcorn spill. Like, a whole family's worth of popcorn. And I think . . . yeah that's throw-up. It's pretty gross."

"We don't have time for that. Audrey, we're gonna need you."

I could see her at the bottom of the sky tunnels, still putting her shoes back on. "Right. You said the guy was tall?"

"He's tall," Conor confirmed.

"OK, then. We'll do Hoops."

"Hoops," Monty repeated, rushing over to the other side of the Starcade where the sports games were. I crawled over to the other lookout point to keep an eye on him. As

Audrey walked over to where Conor was, Monty slotted a token into Hot Shots—the basketball game—grabbed two of the basketballs as they fell, and walked over to the side of the machine. I'd seen teenagers stand over to the side and drop basketballs that a friend handed to them right into the hoop, one after the other for easy points. Instead, Monty placed the balls right in the corner between the hoop and the side so they were stuck.

At the same time, Audrey was walking over to the tall blue shirt near Conor. I could picture her tapping him politely on the shoulder.

"Excuse me," I heard her say over the earbuds. "I was playing the basketball game and the balls got stuck. I'm too short to reach them. Can you please help?"

I could hear him too. Conor must have taken one of his earbuds out so we could listen in. "I'm kind of busy, but I can call someone over."

"It will only take a second," she said, pleading. "And you're so tall. I don't think *anyone* else here is as tall as you."

Even though I couldn't see him, I could tell that the blue shirt puffed a little at that. "I *am* the tallest guy who works here." There was a pause and then, "You know what? I'll help you now."

"Yes! Thank you *sooo* much!"

"Monty, get out of there." He scurried away from the Hot Shots cabinet before Audrey and the blue shirt showed up. I crawled over and checked the Birthday Closet again. "Conor, you're clear. Make the grab."

He dropped the mallet and casually sauntered over to the closet. That's the thing about being sneaky. People think the key to being sneaky is to make yourself small and look over your shoulder and walk like a ninja. That's the exact wrong thing to do most of the time. People don't notice normal behavior. They notice weird behavior. If someone is whispering, you want to know what they're saying. But people are talking around you at a normal level all the time, and do you care what they're saying? No. In fact, you usually tune it out. Acting sneaky is suspicious. Acting casual is sneaky.

Conor did a quick over-the-shoulder glance to make sure there was no one around that I couldn't see and then opened the door.

"Are you kidding me?"

I couldn't see inside the closet. "Conor, what's wrong?"

"It's empty. The closet is empty."

I frowned. We'd known it was a possibility we'd get there between trash runs, but Monty had been pretty confident that we wouldn't. He said he'd never seen them clear out the closet until around ten p.m. when there were so many parties going on.

"Conor, the blue shirt is coming back."

Audrey's voice snapped me out of my thoughts. "Conor, get out of there. Everyone scatter, but be ready to move. We're moving to Plan B."

Plan B counted on us snapping up bags as they came in. It wasn't as good because it meant we had to wait for the machines to fill up, but based on my math, we would be able to snag almost everything we needed with this plan. Conor could get a loan or something if we ended up a couple thousand tickets short. It wasn't ideal, but we still had a plan, and that was what mattered. Still, I had to wonder why the closet was empty. The way the kids were running around like maniacs, there was no way the employees had a ton of extra downtime to take out the trash. This seemed like exactly the kind of day the Birthday Closet was made for.

I scanned the floor again to make sure I had eyes on everyone relevant. Conor was back to playing whack-a-mole. Audrey was talking to one of the girls from the show. Monty was sitting in a racing game booth not too far from her. Then there was the tall blue shirt by the closet. Two more fixing jammed machines. A red shirt by the prize counter and—wait. Gray shirt. Shift manager.

"Heads up, Monty," I said. "Dave is coming by you at six o'clock."

He made a full turn to look, something he couldn't quite stop doing no matter how many times we told him not to.

"Oh no."

Oh no? That wasn't just bad. It was vague, which was almost worse.

"Oh no what? Talk to me, Monty."

"That wasn't Dave. He must have changed his shift. Dave's not working tonight. That's Tony."

Chapter Fourteen
A CHANGE OF PLANS

We needed a team meeting, stat. I called everyone back to base and, while I waited for them to arrive, I kept an eye on Tony. He was stalking between the rows of arcade cabinets with a clipboard, checking things off as he went. Occasionally he would run into one of the other employees on the floor, jab them with the back end of his pencil, and say something. I couldn't tell what he was saying, but it didn't seem like anything you said after jabbing someone with a pencil would be super friendly.

Conor made it back first.

"Well, this makes things more complicated," he said as he crawled back into our little pod.

It wasn't that we hadn't planned for Tony. The plan

had just been to avoid him. "Monty said this guy is a total stickler for the rules. Which explains why the Birthday Closet is empty."

Conor nodded. "He probably has them sending everything to the trash as soon as the bags get full, no matter how busy they are."

I couldn't really blame the guy for wanting the trash to be taken out, but it *really* threw a wrench into our plans. I would have rather convinced Hailey to move her party up a day than have to deal with Tony as the manager on duty, because that meant we had only two obvious options for getting the tickets now: over the barbed wire fence or through the employee-only area. Neither option was ideal.

Monty and Audrey made it back at about the same time, coming from different directions.

"I don't know what he's doing here," Monty said once we were all together. "I'm really sorry. He never changes his shifts, but I should have checked."

I shook my head. "Not your fault. You're new to

this. I should have asked you to confirm. And besides, there's not much we could have done, even if we'd found out earlier this morning. We'd be in pretty much the same position."

"So, what do we do now?" Audrey asked. "The only way we can get the trash tickets now is out of the dumpsters or out of the ticket-counter machines themselves."

"The machines are locked," Conor chimed in. "We'd have to steal the keys off an employee."

"Let's table that," I said. "Monty said his brother got fired for being late after helping a car crash victim. I don't want Tony firing someone because they can't find their keys because we took them."

"I know you said no to this already, but we could always try to grab one of the fresh rolls of tickets from the back," Conor suggested. "If Audrey makes a big enough distraction, I can get back there and—"

"No," I said firmly. "You know those aren't the tickets we came for. Besides, the rolls of tickets are smooth before they go through the machines. If anyone gets suspicious and looks at them, the fact that they don't have the little bumps on them from going through the machines will be a dead giveaway."

"So that leaves the dumpster," Audrey said. "But I thought that was a dead end."

"Maybe it is," I said. "But we don't know. We planned around it because that was easier, but there might be a way we haven't thought of yet. Now that we're on location, it will be easier to tell. Like, maybe there's a gap in the fence outside or something. Conor and I will go check it out. You two wait here."

They nodded, and Conor followed behind me. We went down the slide and put our shoes back on. Then, we pushed our party wristbands up as far as they would go and hid them under our sleeves.

"I've actually been thinking about it," Conor said as we walked toward the exit. "If we had something to put over the spikes, like maybe a thick jacket or something, maybe we could get over the fence. And, if we need to go through the employee area, I have some stuff that might help with a distraction. Fake blood capsules from my sister's vampire costume and liquid fart spray."

I wrinkled my nose. That fart spray stuff was military-grade gross. I honestly didn't know why they were allowed to sell it to kids online.

"That's good, but let's just check out the fence first and go from there."

There was only the one way in and out of the Starcade for guests, and now, there was a blue-shirt standing there, stamping kids and adults as they came in. According to the employee's manual, she was supposed to check every kid who left the building, but after watching her for a minute, I saw that she wasn't. She let a lot of older-looking kids by her without a word. Probably not great for security, but good for us.

As we approached the door, I didn't avoid eye contact with her, but I also didn't look at her on purpose. Like I said before, the best way to be sneaky is to not be.

"Hey. You two boys."

Of course, nothing is foolproof.

I could see Conor priming to bolt but I caught his eye. This wasn't a situation for running. He relaxed and let me talk.

"Yes?" I said innocently.

"Where are you guys' parents?" she asked.

"They dropped us off."

"How old are you?"

"We're in middle school," I said, not really answering the question as I kept moving. Unfortunately, she was already drawing her UV penlight and shining it in our direction. As soon as she caught the telltale glow of a UV stamp on the back of my hand, she had me dead to rights.

"You're under thirteen," she said, before catching Conor's hand, which he didn't bother to hide at that point.

"Yeah, we just wanted to go outside for a sec to—"

She stopped me in my tracks. "I'm sorry. I can't let you guys leave without your parents. Liability reasons."

"That's all right," I said, pulling on Conor's sleeve. "Let's go play Skee-Ball." When we were far enough away I said, "They wouldn't let us pass," even though I was pretty sure they'd figured that out from what they'd heard over comms. "What about you, Audrey? Aren't you thirteen?"

"I am," she said, "But they won't let me leave either with the party bracelet on. I'm stuck in here with you guys until the two hours are up."

"Do you think you can cook up some sob story so they'll make an exception for you? Or we could cut it off for now. Or you could borrow my hoodie and hide it under your sleeve."

"I could," she said. "But I don't think I have to. Why not just send Monty? He looks like he's in high school. They probably won't even check him for a stamp."

"Unless they know him," I pointed out. "His brother used to work here. Don't the staff know you here?"

"Some of the red shirts," said Monty. "But I think most of the blue shirts that were working here when I used to come here are gone. They don't stay very long."

"Great," said Conor. "Then you can go out and scout for us."

"By myself?" he said, a note of tension in his voice.

"Don't worry," I said. "You just need to go out there and tell us what you see. Even better, you can take pictures so we can see for ourselves. Super simple."

"I guess," he said, but he didn't sound very convinced. I was about to try to say something encouraging when Audrey piped in.

"I know you don't wanna go alone, but we'll be on comms the whole time," she said soothingly. "You just need to walk out, look around, and walk back in. Just three things. And, if anything happens, we'll bail you out. OK?"

There was a little pause and then he said, "OK. OK, yeah. I can do it."

I wished Audrey was close by so I could flash her a quick good-job thumbs-up, but that would have to wait. Instead, I watched the slide of the sky tunnels until I saw Monty slide down and put his shoes back on.

He walked over to the entrance, a little more nervously than I would have liked, but not enough that he was screaming, "HEY, SOMETHING'S UP!" with his body language. As he walked by, the blue shirt at the front desk shot him a quick glance but didn't ask to see his wrist.

He breathed a huge sigh of relief as he made it out the doors.

"Good job," I said. "Now just go to the alley and take a look around."

"Right." The evening breeze whipped in his mic and made him harder to hear. "Uh, OK. I'm at the fence."

"How does it look?" asked Conor.

"It's locked and it's pretty high. Like, seven feet? Eight with the barbed wire."

"Does the wire cover the entire fence?" I asked.

"Yeah. I'll take a picture for you guys." There was another small pause and then all our phones pinged at once. The picture proved Monty's sparse description completely accurate. It was just a tall, barbed wire fence. No gap, no slack, no obvious way to get over it.

"Can you take a close-up picture of the lock?" Conor asked.

"Sure." He took one and sent it over. I took a quick look at it, but I knew that if anyone was going to be able to do anything with it, it would be Conor. I looked over at him.

He shook his head. "Sorry. Not my kind of lock. But maybe I could snag the key if we could figure out who has it?"

It was a better plan than bolt cutters, but I still didn't love the idea of key stealing. On the other hand, I didn't have any other bright ideas.

"OK, Monty, you did good. Come back and we'll circle up to figure out what we're doing next."

"On my way."

Conor and I hung around the Skee-Ball machine for long enough to make sure Monty got back in OK. Once he did, I said, "OK, Monty, you get up to base with Audrey first. Once you're up, Conor will follow and then me."

Monty was already on his way to the sky tunnels. He started taking his shoes off, but before he could put them in the little cubby, Audrey said, "Monty, don't freak, everything's fine, but Tony's coming right for you."

"What?" I could hear the panic rising in his voice. "But I thought you said it was fine!"

"It is fine," I said. "Just shush. You look like you're talking to yourself." At the same time, I motioned for Conor to run over to him. "I'm sending Conor over to listen in, and, Audrey, be ready to bail him out."

"Got it," she said.

"Just act natural," I said to Monty, right as Tony reached him. I saw Conor sneak up, take out one of his earbuds, and hold it up so Audrey and I could hear the other side of the conversation.

"Hey, you!" he snapped at Monty's ear and Monty jumped. I frowned automatically. People who snap at other people are, in my experience, across-the-board terrible.

Monty turned around, almost sheepishly, as if he'd been caught red-handed stuffing a roll of tickets into his jeans.

Tony stood a touch taller than Monty, but Monty was slouching into himself and Tony looked like he was trying to make every inch count as an inch and a half. His pants were crisply pressed, his hair was neatly parted, and he was squinting at Monty from behind his glasses.

"I thought it was you," Tony barked. Monty's brother was right. He did talk like he was a five-star general and not a glorified babysitter. "Where's Felix?"

"He's, uh, he's not here. I got dropped off by a friend's mom."

"Good," he said, jabbing a finger as close to Monty's chest as he could without technically touching him. "Because he's still banned for life, and if he sets one single foot into this building, I'm going to call the cops so fast his head will spin. You tell him that."

"You've got to be kidding me," Audrey said, and I could picture her face scrunching in disgust even though I couldn't see her.

"Yeah, I, uh, I'll tell him, I guess."

"You do that," he said. "And if you get any ideas about testing me like your brother who thought he was so smart, don't think I'll go easy on you because you're a kid."

"Please let me fart spray this guy," Conor said quietly.

I shushed him, even though I was tempted to let him.

Monty shook his head. "I don't think I'm smart. I

mean, I'm not like my brother. I mean—I'm just going up." He tried to stick his shoes into an open cubby, but Tony stopped him.

"What do you think you're doing?"

"Going in the sky tunnels?"

Tony slapped the height chart just outside the sky tunnels entrance. "You know the rules. You must be this short to enter." Even from a distance I could see that Monty was way taller than the sign. Tony squinted at Monty suspiciously. "I've never seen you play in the sky tunnels before. What are you doing in there all of a sudden?"

"Uhh . . ."

"Hang on, Monty," Audrey said over comms. A few seconds later, I saw her popping out of the slide. She came up to Tony from behind and tugged on the back of his shirt.

"Excuse me," she said, fidgeting with her sleeves and keeping her eyes at the floor like she was too shy to look at him straight on. "Can you show me where the bathroom is?"

"Huh? Oh, it's over there."

"Over there?" she said pointing to the kitchen entrance.

"No, there."

"There?" she said, pointing at the door to a utility closet.

"No, it's . . ." His face twitched with annoyance. "I'll just show you. Come on." He looked at Monty over his shoulder before bringing Audrey toward the bathroom.

"Monty, get out of there," I said as Audrey lured Tony away. He skittered off, shoes in hand. "Conor, you too. We don't want to get caught together. And especially not with Monty. It looks like he's watching you extra close."

"He doesn't like me because of my brother," Monty said. "He always watches me like he thinks I'm up to something."

"Well, that's gonna be a problem," Conor said. "As if we don't have enough of those."

"Heads up," Audrey said. "He's on his way back."

I made myself scarce but stuck close enough that I would still have line of sight when Tony returned. When he came back, he glanced over to where Monty had been and frowned. He scanned the room before pulling out a walkie-talkie and saying something into it. I did my best to read his lips.

"Yo, he said something in his walkie," Conor said. "Did you catch that?"

"Not all of it," I said. "But he for sure said 'Monty' and 'tunnels.' I think he told whoever he was talking to to make sure Monty stays out of the sky tunnels."

"This dude makes Javert look all warm and cuddly," Audrey griped. "Why does he even care so much?"

"This is my fault," Monty said miserably. "I should just call my brother and get him to pick me up so I don't ruin anything else."

"No," I said, shaking my head. "You haven't messed anything up. This makes things more complicated, but we just need to think of a new strategy." I glanced over at where Tony was standing watch over the sky tunnels like he had Terminator vision. "And we need to do something about him."

Chapter Fifteen
BLOODY BUSINESS

Even in the middle of the most important job, life goes on and so do birthday parties. About five minutes after Monty's run-in with Tony, there was an announcement over the loudspeaker that pizza was ready. It was time we could have used, but I knew that Hailey or her mom would come look for us if we didn't show up, and we didn't need to draw attention to ourselves. Monty wasn't allowed into the party area, but that was OK. While Tony was watching the sky tunnels for him, we'd sent him outside again. If he was so dead set on finding Monty, he was gonna be looking for a long time.

We were one member down, but we were still on

mission and time was still ticking. We were a quarter of the way through our two hours.

"This dude saw Monty across a crowded room when he wasn't even looking for him," Conor said, a long strand of pizza cheese hanging from his mouth. "Now that he knows he's here, he's gonna be basically stalking him. We won't be able to stealthily move him anywhere."

"Won't be able to move him stealthily without a distraction," Audrey corrected. "But isn't that the whole reason I'm here?"

I handed Conor a napkin. "Yeah, but you're like a rifle with a scope. That was fine for the closet but the closet's out. We need a bazooka to pull this new plan off. This has got to be bigger than anything you can do alone."

"If you're nixing our ideas, I hope that means you have one," Conor said over another mouthful of pizza.

I held up my phone and nodded. "To start, we fight fire with fire. Monty got us the employee handbook. If this guy is such a stickler for the rules, we use the rules against him. There's got to be something in here that will get him away from whatever we're doing. You guys have copies. Help me look."

They did.

"How about this?" Audrey said. "It says the head manager on duty has to break up fights."

"I could fake a fight," Conor chimed in. "That's how I got transferred to the Fitz."

"He could kick us out for that," I said. "It has to be big, but not so big that we get kicked out."

"Good point."

We did some more scrolling.

"Oh," Audrey said after another minute. "What about this? It says that any child who is injured on the premises has to be checked out by the manager on duty for legal reasons. I guess so they don't get sued."

"That's good. That could be our in. Actually—Conor. Didn't you say you had those blood capsules?"

He patted his pocket with excitement. "Yeah, I have a ton. I could bite down on a bunch of them in front of him and cough them up. He'll freak!"

"Yeah, because coughing up blood is what people do before they *die*. We don't want him to think you have tuberculosis."

"He won't think that. I can just say I ran into something and knocked out a tooth."

"What if he asks to see the tooth?"

"Dude, why would I stop and look for a missing tooth if I was bleeding everywhere?"

"So you could put it in milk and get to the dentist to put it back in."

"That works?"

"What about a bloody nose?" Audrey said suddenly.

"Huh?" Conor said, but I was already right with her.

"That's perfect. A lot of blood, but not serious. No reason to call nine-one-one. We'd just have to crack the capsules beforehand, get some napkins really fake bloody. Really sell that this is *the best birthday party I've ever been to*," I finished loudly.

"Aww, thanks, Flounder," Hailey said. "Glad you're having a good time." My back was to Hailey, but I had spotted her coming toward us in the shiny balloon I was using to keep an eye on things. "I came to see if you guys wanted more pizza. We have a ton of extra. My mom ordered way too much."

"Nah, we're good, I think." I could see Conor about to open his mouth, but I gave him a look that said, *You can have more pizza when we're done saving your butt*, and he sank back into his chair without saying anything.

"OK, cool. Lemme know if you change your minds. We'll need to clear the pizza away before cake. Well, it's going to be pizza, karaoke, then cake, so you have some time, but don't wait too long or it'll get cold. And I . . ." Hailey suddenly stopped and squinted.

"What?" I said.

"I feel like I've seen that kid over there before. Does he go to our school?"

I turned my head, thinking I'd see Monty back on the floor unexpectedly early, but it wasn't him. It was Duke. But what was he doing here? Clearly Hailey hadn't invited him to her party. And he lived across town like the rest of us. If he wanted to go to a Starcade, he could go to the one next to school. He was standing on his tiptoes and looking around, like a kid who'd lost his mom at the mall. I quickly turned back around.

"Maybe," I lied. "I can't tell from this far away."

"Hmm. Whatever. Anyway, you have some time now if you want to play some more games, but you have to be back for karaoke, OK?" She nudged Audrey. "Birthday girl rules. Everyone has to sing."

"We'll be back," Audrey assured her.

"And eat more pizza!"

"We will! You don't have to babysit us to be a good host." She playfully lowered her voice. "And I know you're only going table to table checking on people so you have an excuse to talk to you-know-who."

Hailey blushed slightly, but she didn't look embarrassed.

"I'll see you guys in ten," she said with a smile before glancing over at Tyler and beelining for his table.

I watched to make sure she was out of earshot before turning back to the group.

"Do you guys have any idea why Duke would be here?" I asked.

"Duke?" Conor asked. "You mean the kid who tripped the alarm in the library to stop the announcements for you?"

"He's not friends with Hailey, that's for sure," Audrey said. "Maybe it's just a coincidence?"

"Maybe, but I doubt it." I shook my head. "It's fine. Just one more thing to keep track of. Conor, keep an eye on him."

"Got it."

I scanned the game floor. Tony was doing the same thing, posted near the hallway that led to the employee-only area, the hallway that led back to the alley and the dumpster full of tickets. I turned back to the plan at hand.

"OK, here's what we're doing. I'll be the distraction to draw him away from the hallway. Audrey, you're our panic button. I want you to hang back and swoop in if things get too crazy. Just improv."

She nodded. "I can do that."

"Conor, while I'm distracting him, you make for the hallway."

He struck a ninja pose. "I am a shadow."

I rolled my eyes. "Just do your job. And help out with these capsules. What's the best way to do this?"

"You just cut the tip and bite down. But you want a nose bleed so . . . here." He grabbed a napkin and took out a pocket knife. Then he cut the tip off one of the pellets. It came out super thick, almost like finger paint. "We should thin this out a little. I think it usually thins when it mixes with spit, but we can use water."

He ran over to the soda dispenser, poured out what was in his cup, and filled it with about half an inch of water. When he came back, he squeezed in the fake blood and mixed it with his straw. Then, he transferred the thinned fake blood onto the napkin with the straw, like he was making one of those famous splatter paintings. After about a minute, it was good and fake-bloody.

"Here," he said, handing it to me under the table. "You can hold it up to your nose and hold an open capsule under it. Then you can squeeze it and make it drip blood."

He took one of the empty capsules we'd used and filled it with the thinned mixture. "Be careful with that. I think this stuff washes out, but you still don't want to get it everywhere."

I took it carefully and held it under the napkin, which I held at my side. Then I adjusted my comms. "Everyone know what they're doing?"

"Yeah," said Conor.

"I think so," said Monty.

"I'm ready," said Audrey.

"Good. And you're the lookout, so you should go first. Stand by the prize counter and pretend like you're deciding what to get. We'll follow in thirty seconds."

Audrey nodded. "Right. Good luck."

I watched her casually dump her empty paper plate and saunter toward the counter.

"Hey," Conor said. "Do you really think this is going to work? I mean, we've done complicated before, but this is pretty out there. And not even on our home turf."

I didn't take my eyes off Audrey. She was in position. "It's risky," I admitted. "But I think we can pull it off. The four of us." I scanned the room one more time and took a deep breath. "I'm going in. Conor, do your thing when you see an opening."

I slipped out of the booth, napkin clutched in one hand, blood capsule in the other. I didn't want any of the adults in the party area to see it and stop me before I got to my target. Once I was out of range, I held it up to my nose, and held the capsule upside down under it with my other hand, my fingertips keeping the opening pinched shut.

Tony hadn't moved from his spot, and his careful survey of the floor meant he would see Conor right away if he went for the hall behind him. Which is why I had to draw his attention. I was up at bat.

I dug up the memory of the time I crashed my bike into a tree and lost a baby tooth as inspiration and then stumbled over to Tony.

"Uh, yo. Are you in charge?" He looked down and flinched back when he saw me.

"What happened?" He looked equal parts horrified and hypnotized by the amount of fake blood saturating the napkin.

"I dunno. I didn't think I hit the wall that hard. Do you know how to stop a nosebleed?"

"Yes, uh, I, uh, pinch the bridge of your nose." I pretended to do that, but, instead, I squeezed the blood capsule so more fake blood spurted into my hands and over the napkin.

He quickly scrambled toward the nearest napkin dispenser, grabbed a handful, and shoved them toward me. "Here, here. The bathroom is this way. Come on." As I followed him toward the bathroom, I saw Conor slip past us and make his way for the spot where Tony had just been standing.

Conor was as much of a ninja as he promised. Between his stealth and my distraction, Tony didn't notice him at all. And he probably wouldn't have either if Monty hadn't walked in at that exact moment.

"Heads up," Audrey said over comms.

I turned around, almost without thinking and there he was, just past reception and a head taller than anyone else, like a Canadian lighthouse.

"Hey," Tony said. "Don't spray the blood everywh—" He stopped abruptly as he spotted Monty. That's not where we needed him looking. I squirted out the last of the blood and let it dribble down my upper lip.

"Uh, dude. I'm still bleeding."

His line of sight moved reluctantly away from Monty and toward me. But you know who was also moving toward me? Mr. Ninja.

"Hey!" Tony barked. Conor jumped like a jackrabbit. "What are you doing?"

"Looking for the bathroom," he said. His default lie.

"The sign says employees only," Tony said, sounding suspicious.

"There's a sign?" Conor said, standing next to the big, block-lettered sign at eye level. Tony looked at him, looked at it, and then looked at him again.

"Yes."

"Oh, totally my bad. Sorry, dude." And then he bailed, walking past the bathrooms without stopping.

After about a second, Tony started us toward the bathroom again. I couldn't see Monty and Conor, but I knew they were together because I could hear them over the comms.

"What did I miss? Did you guys get the tickets?"

"Shh!" Conor said.

I hated to micromanage when things were already so dicey, but I couldn't help but turn around. They were standing out in the open where anyone could see them talking. And anyone watching me could watch me watching them. I turned back quickly, but I could tell Tony was turning behind me. If he was looking where I had just been looking, he would see them talking. I kept my eyes straight ahead for the rest of the short walk to the bathroom.

Tony helped me clean up and I threw out the capsule with the napkins. At that point, I was miraculously not bleeding anymore and OK to go back on the floor. Before we did, Tony stopped me.

"Do you happen to know that kid I just talked to? The one who said he was looking for the bathroom?"

"Nope," I lied.

"Hmm. OK." And then he left.

I took a few deep breaths. Then I said, "Status report, guys. Are you clear?"

"Tony's coming back my way from the bathroom," Audrey said.

"I put Monty in one of the photo booths," Conor said. "Out of sight but all up in Tony's mind hopefully."

"Did I screw that up?" Monty said from wherever Conor had stashed him. I could practically hear him nervously wringing his hands over the phone. He and Audrey were both newbies, but Audrey was cool under pressure. Monty clearly needed to be babysat.

"You did fine," I said, doing my best to copy Audrey's calming tone from earlier. "Just try to keep a low profile for the rest of the night. Conor, you too. We don't want to lay it on too thick."

"Aye, aye, Captain."

I rolled my eyes. "I need to wash a stain out of my shirt before it sets. Hold tight and I'll be back on the floor in two."

That only gave me a two-minute break before I needed to figure out our next step to keep the plan on track.

Well, one minute actually.

I also had to deal with the stain.

Chapter Sixteen
THE ACE

I came out of the bathroom with a clean shirt and our next step.

"OK, guys," I said. "Spread out. I want you guys looking for someone who's cleaning up. Like, a string of tickets from here back to school. Best player in the arcade."

"Don't you think it's a little late to try to recruit a ringer?" Conor said. "I didn't think we were still trying the 'win the tickets' thing."

"We're not," I said. "But a lot of winning means a lot of tickets, which means someone has to come over and refill the dispenser. And if we play our cards right, that person will be Tony."

"Which frees one of us up to do another run at the

employees-only hallway," Conor said. "Cool. Oh, and, Monty? I'm gonna need that spray back if you're done with it. Just stick it in your back pocket and I'll walk past and swipe it."

"I can just give it back to you."

"Nah, it's sneakier that way."

"That, and Conor's a drama queen," I said. "Just let him have this one, Monty."

We fanned out, each taking a quadrant of the room. I was in the corner with most of the kiddie games. No one was exactly cleaning up and, with the low-ticket payout, not even a toddler with the reflexes of a pro gamer could pick up more than five or six at a time.

"Nothing over here," I said. "What about you guys?"

"Nothing here either," Conor said.

"I think I see someone," Monty said. "By the Skee-Ball lanes on the far end."

"Oh," said Audrey. "I think we're looking at the same person. Blond girl. Like, a teenager but older? Maybe college age?"

"Yeah," he said. "She has a lot of tickets coming out of her machine."

"He's right. It looks like five hundred easy. And she's not using one of the bags from here. She has a trash bag, like she knew she was going to need it so she brought it from home."

That was exactly what we were looking for. If they weren't exaggerating, she might clean out the machine soon without us even having to do anything. But it wasn't just cleaning it out. The timing needed to be right. And we needed Audrey to make sure it went down properly.

"Great. Do you think you can sweet-talk her into a couple of things?"

"Oh yeah. Just give me, like, two minutes. Three tops— Hailey!" she said abruptly.

"Audrey?" I said.

I could hear Hailey say something faintly in the background and then Audrey said, "Yeah, I know we said we'd be back for karaoke but—" She was cut off. More background talk. "Oh, you want me to do a duet with Conor."

"Oh man," Conor said. "You guys told her she likes me. Hailey's trying to set it up. I'm going for the sky tunnels."

"I'm sure he's around here somewhere," Audrey said to Hailey.

"Ha. Not for long," Conor said.

"Wait," I said. "You don't know Hailey. She's like a dog with a bone. She'll track you down, and we're trying to avoid suspicious disappearances. We want Hailey to remember that you guys were right on time to karaoke if someone shakes her down later, not that she randomly couldn't find you in the middle of her party when you were supposed to be around."

"So you want me to go do it?"

"Yeah. We're on a tight timeline, but we can handle the couple of minutes it's gonna take for you to sing one song. Then, when you leave together, Hailey will just think her plan worked and you guys are chilling. Me and Monty can keep an eye on the blond ace while you're gone."

"If you say so. I'm by the Pac-Man machine, Audrey."

"Oh, there he is," Audrey said to Hailey. "Hey, Conor! Over here!"

They kept talking but I let it fade into background noise as I headed over to the Skee-Ball machines where Monty and Audrey had spotted the high roller.

Their descriptions had been accurate. The girl at the machine had her hair clipped out of her eyes and was staring at the screen like she was trying to laser blast right through it. She did look around college age, and there did look like there were at least five hundred tickets coming out of her machine. I thought the game looked familiar, and after a second, I realized why. It was Rowdy Roundup, the same farm game the guy at the other Starcade had been playing. I slotted a token into the Skee-Ball machine across from where she was standing so I could watch her out of the corner of my eye.

Just like the guy at the Starcade near school, she was clearing her boards slowly, but she was racking up the points quickly. She was finishing up a game when I started watching her, and when she was done, the machine spit out another hundred tickets, easy. Based on the way the machine was flashing, she'd broken some kind of record. She ripped the tickets and shoved them into her mostly full trash bag. Then she looked around the game floor.

"I think she might be on the move," I said to Monty. "I'll let you know if she goes in your direc—" I trailed off as I saw the girl check her watch and then glance at the door. "Shoot, no. She's getting ready to leave. We need to cut her off now." Over comms, I could hear Audrey and Conor singing some duet from a Disney movie that had come out last year. There were still a good two minutes left in the song and this girl was already moving for the door. I couldn't wait for Audrey to do her thing. "I'm going in. Audrey, come back me up as soon as you can."

As I walked toward her, I didn't know what I was going to say. I did big-picture planning and a simple distraction or two. Not major Face stuff. I knew the kind of things people wanted to hear, not the exact words to say. But it was either me or Monty, and he definitely wasn't a talker.

I just needed to hold her for two minutes. Then Audrey could bail me out and—

"Before you ask, no."

"Huh?" It was a genuine reaction. I wasn't expecting her to get the jump on me. I didn't think she'd noticed me at all.

"And you're not going to make me feel guilty about it either," she said, hoisting the bag of tickets over her shoulder. "So don't call your mom over to yell at me. I don't work for free."

Ah! Now she was speaking my language. "I wasn't going to say that."

She raised an eyebrow. "Oh, so you haven't been eyeing me for the past two minutes?"

"You noticed?"

"I spend a lot of time in this arcade. I can tell when some kid is watching a hot streak over my shoulder."

Fair enough. "I was watching you," I admitted. "But I wasn't going to ask for free tickets. Quid pro quo, right? If I want something, I have to give you something."

She snorted. "What, do you have a whole pitch ready?"

"No. But I do have twenty tokens. And based on how good you've been playing, I think they're worth a lot more to you than they would be to me."

For the first time in the conversation, her posture shifted. She put one hand on her hip and really looked at me, like she was taking the conversation seriously. "You want all of these tickets for twenty tokens?"

"No. I'll give you all of these tokens if you play them all in that machine, right now."

"Wait, what do you get out of that?"

"Does it matter?"

"I'm curious, yeah."

My brain spit out ten lies and grabbed the best one. "You're really good. I wanna watch what you do. See if I can learn something."

Her relaxed posture shifted back into an on-the-move one. "Sorry, kid. I don't have time to teach a class. Next time, catch me earlier. I have to go."

I was losing her. I had to say something to get her to stay. I had to connect.

"Wait! I want you to drain the machine." When she stopped, I quickly added, "Of tickets, I mean. Empty it out."

Her hand found its way back to her hip. "Why?"

The truth seemed to be working and it was easy enough to deny later. I decided to stick with it. "If you empty it out, someone will have to come over and refill it. I want to distract someone who works here."

"Who?"

She was a regular here. She had to be, based on the way she talked and the way she played. I took a chance.

"Tony." The involuntary twitch of disgust from her face was exactly the reaction I'd been hoping for. "You know him."

"Ugh. Yeah, I know him. I hate that guy. The first time I came in here and scored a bunch of jackpots on the Bunny Slope machine, he reset the machine settings and made me play a game in front of him to prove I hadn't somehow messed with them. Like, first of all, how dare you, and *second* of all, I'm a gamer, not a hacker. I wouldn't even know how to do that. And I know a lot of the APs who hit this place up. Does he ask any of the dudes? No, of course not. But if a girl is breaking records, she has to be cheating." She pounded a fist into the side of the nearest cabinet and grimaced.

"He fired my friend's brother," I said.

"Oh, the Canadian guy?" Her face softened slightly. "I liked him. He never argued with me when machines ate my tokens, and he let me know when good prizes were coming in. Is that why he doesn't work here anymore?"

"That's what he said."

"Ugh. What a tool. So, what? Are you pranking him or something?"

Not quite. "I don't want to get too into it, but, if it works, he's gonna feel pretty stupid by the time I leave."

The girl glanced at the door, glanced at her watch, and then looked back at me. She was right on the edge, I could feel it. She just needed a nudge.

"I have more tokens. I can double it. Make it forty."

"I don't need more tokens. And I am actually in a

rush. I wasn't even going to run these tickets through the counter today. Even as good as I am—and I'm very good—it would take a while to drain a machine. But you just want to distract him, right?"

"Basically, yeah."

"Then I have an idea. Follow me."

I did. And, as I walked, I had an idea of my own.

"Monty," I whispered, letting myself fall a little behind her. "Go to the bathroom. I need you to make a call."

Chapter Seventeen
DUKE IT OUT

Audrey and Conor got out of their karaoke duties a few minutes later and checked in over comms.

"Sorry about that," Audrey said. "But I heard everything. You didn't need us at all. That was fantastic. I don't think I would have thought of all that."

"Yeah, well, if someone wants the same thing you do, you don't have to sweet-talk them. You can just ask them outright."

I was standing in front of a game called Silver Star. It was a VR shooter.

"They're testing out VR cabinets in the bigger Starcades," Laura, the blond ace, had said earlier. "Batter Up and the Harry Potter knock-off where you cast spells are pretty good, but this one is super buggy. The saloon level is pretty much unplayable. If you just stand still for, like, ten seconds and don't shoot anything, the game freaks out and crashes. Tony will have to come over and put his code in to restart the machine."

"Audrey, I'm at the game. You need to switch off with me."

"I'll be right there."

I took off the VR headset and set it down on its holder. A second later, Audrey smoothly came up behind me, put in two tokens, and started playing.

"Remember, pick the saloon level. Don't shoot."

"I remember, DJ," she singsonged. "My part here is easy. Concentrate on the rest of it."

"Right. Conor, is Tony still following Monty around?" Conor was in the sky tunnels, keeping a bird's-eye view for us.

"Yup. Just a couple of feet back. He's pretending like he's checking on the machines. He's not super stealthy, believe it or not."

"Great. Audrey?"

"In the saloon. Five seconds."

"OK, Monty. Start walking in her direction. Conor, meet me on the floor."

"Got it."

"Oh! Ow!" Audrey hissed over the line. "She wasn't kidding. It's totally glitching out. I have to take these goggles off, my eyes hurt."

I could see Monty rounding the corner with Tony not too far behind.

"Take them off, Audrey. You're up."

I watched her snatch the goggles off and run up to Tony, making him jump, he was so caught up in watching Monty.

"Oh, good. I was about to go look for you."

He looked over her head, trying to keep track of where Monty was. "One second, I—"

"The shooting game is broken," Audrey said insistently. "The lights went all flashy."

"That's good, Monty. Come over to where I am." He

did, coming to stand by me, just across from the Silver Star machine. When Tony saw that, his face went tight with suspicion.

"My eyes really hurt," Audrey continued, with a nuclear-grade pout. "And it took my tokens."

Conor slid up to my other side, with his arms crossed.

"You sure this is a good idea?" he said. The three of us were standing across from Audrey and Tony like birds on a telephone line, and Tony wasn't taking his eyes off us. That was fine. I stared right back at him.

"Trust me," I said. "Audrey, hook him."

Her voice suddenly got high and tight. "Oh my gosh! What if I go blind? I saw that in a movie once. What if they have to take out one of my eyes and I have to wear an eye patch! I can't pull off an eye patch!"

People were starting to stare. Tony quickly started shushing her.

"Hey, hey, hey. You're not going to go blind. Here, I'll fix the machine. Watch."

He started messing with the machine, but every few

seconds, he'd glance back over to where we were standing. After a few seconds, I finally broke my stare to look over at Conor.

"Now."

He gave me a little salute and darted away. From the direction he was walking, it was pretty clear he was going for the employee-only hallway, but there wasn't much Tony could do about it right away. He had his hands full with Audrey, and she was making talking to her a full-time job.

"What's wrong with the machine? How long will it take to fix? Can I still play it? Do you think I should get my eyes tested?" She machine-gunned questions at him faster than most people could understand, let alone answer, as Conor slipped away.

Tony was working that machine like he was on an Indy 500 pit crew, but I had faith in Conor. When Tony lost line of sight, he grabbed his walkie-talkie and said something I couldn't hear over comms.

"Heads up," I said to Conor. "You might have some blue shirts coming your way."

He scoffed. "And? What are they gonna do?"

"Conor."

"All right, all right. I'll be careful."

"That kid is watching us," Monty said suddenly.

"Huh? Who?" He started to point, but I grabbed his hand. "No, just tell me where."

"To the left, at the fishing game."

I checked out of the corner of my eye. Duke again. He was playing the game with one hand and holding his phone with the other, camera out in our direction. I'd almost forgotten about him.

"All right, circling back now," Conor said, snapping me back to what we were doing. In my head, I put dealing with Duke next on my to-do list.

As quickly as he'd melted into the crowd, Conor reappeared, flashing me a big thumbs-up. I pushed his hand back down to his side.

"All right, Audrey," I said. "Conor's back. You can bail when you're ready. Everyone else, split off on three. One, two, three."

Conor and Monty fell back and walked off in opposite directions. I stood in place. A few seconds in, I pulled out my phone and held it up high like I was taking a picture of myself. Really, I just wanted to see what was going on behind me. Duke was still watching me.

I casually walked over to him and took the machine next to his.

"Hey, Duke," I said lightly. "Watchu doing?"

"Oh, hey, DJ," he said, suddenly very interested in his screen. "Just playing a game."

"Really? Because they have this exact same game at the Starcade right next to school. You could have gone there."

"*You* could have gone there," he said.

"I'm at a party," I shot back. "One I know you weren't invited to. But I guess you just wanted a change of scenery, right? Maybe you're shooting video for your YouTube prank channel."

"Ah, yeah!" he said, latching on to the idea. "You know what I do."

"Yeah, I do." Which was the truth. I did know what he did: anything for fifty tickets on a dare. "Delete it," I said.

"Delete what?"

"You know what. Delete it. All of it." I moved over to the other side of the machine to force him to look at me. "A thousand tickets right now if you get rid of all of it."

His eyes flashed with greed for a moment before he said, "Sorry, man. I don't know what you're talking about."

"Two thousand tickets."

"I don't—"

"Ten thousand."

"Look, man, I don't—"

Suddenly, I felt a shadow fall over me. At first, I thought it was Tony, but, when I saw the frightened-bunny look on Duke's face, I knew I was wrong.

"Delete the footage," I tried again, with an extra dose of threat behind the words.

This time, Duke tripped over his words when he talked. "Come on, man. I'd do it if I could. I mean, for ten thousand tickets? You know me. I would. But I can't. Anything else, I'm your guy, but I can't do that." His eyes flicked nervously above my head and then back to my eyes.

"Can't, huh?" I looked him over again. He didn't look like he was messing with me. In fact, he looked like he wanted to go to the bathroom and change his underwear. "OK, fine. New deal. I'm not gonna fight you for that footage. But whatever you take, I want it too. All of it. You get me?" He nodded, quickly. "Good. I'll tell you where to send it later." I was about to walk away but I saw his lips twitching, like he wanted to ask a question but wasn't sure how to. "What?"

"Do I still get the ten thousand tickets?"

I rolled my eyes. "Come on, Monty. Let's go." I waited until there was a little distance between us and Duke before I said, "Way to come in clutch, man. No one even had to call you in."

"You said my job was to stand around and look tough. I thought it might help."

I gave him a little nudge. "It totally did. See? I told you you were helping. Now go lay low until we need you."

He nodded happily and walked off. I was about to do the same when I felt another shadow fall over me. And, this time, when I turned around, it wasn't an ally there to have my back. It was the exact opposite.

Chapter Eighteen
NOT-SO-SMOOTH CRIMINAL

Some people think someone threatening you outright is the scariest thing that can happen to you. I think they're wrong. Nothing is scarier than what you don't know—and someone looking at you, eyes overflowing with suspicion but mouth zipped shut, is the absolute worst.

But I couldn't let that show on my face. Jumpy insides, calm outsides. So, instead, I just stopped short and said, "Whoa, I almost bumped into you. Sorry about that."

Tony looked down at me, eyes narrowed with suspicion, nose twitching like he'd just gotten a whiff of spoiled milk. "I know what you're doing here," he said, his voice tight and even.

"Yeah," I said. "My name's on the list for the party." I perked up. "Oh! Do you think the cake got cut yet?"

Oh, he did *not* like that. "I saw you," he snapped. "You thought you were being sneaky, but I saw you talking to that boy you said you didn't know."

"Met him today. Seems like a cool guy."

"And I heard him talking to Monty. About getting tickets."

"That's what you do at an arcade, isn't it?"

He frowned. "I don't know who you think you are, but you come into my arcade and try to lie to my face and talk to me like I was born yesterday. I should throw you out right now. Both of you and the other one. You're all in on it together, aren't you?" He did his impression of sympathy. "Why don't you just tell me what you did, and then I won't have to do something drastic."

"I just told you what I've been doing. Playing video games."

His face said he would have slapped me if we weren't surrounded by people. He got close to my face, so close that I could hear him over the craziness of the arcade, even though he'd dropped down to a hiss.

"I saw him. I saw him sneak back there to go take tickets."

I dropped the clueless act for a second, looked him right in the eye, and said, "If he stole tickets, where are they?" I held out my empty palms and took a step back.

He moved to close the distance again. "If you don't think I'll figure out where you hid them, then—"

"Flounder!" Hailey suddenly tackled me from behind and draped herself over me. "Audrey said you were trying to ditch out on karaoke!"

In the time it took Tony to blink, I was a clueless kid again. "Me? Ditch? No way. I was just in the middle of a really important conver—"

She didn't even let me finish. "Oh please. You're not getting out of it that easy. Let's go. Birthday girl rules." She grabbed my collar and started dragging me toward the party.

"Birthday girl rules," I called back to Tony with a *What*

can I do? shrug. He looked furious, but he didn't follow us.

"Just for that, I'm going to make you sing something super embarrassing," she said, eyes lit up with teasing mischief.

"What? Come on, Ariel!"

"Nuh-uh. Cute set nicknames aren't gonna save you. Take your punishment with dignity."

As we crossed back into the party area, I saw Audrey, sitting off to the side at one of the tables. "Thank you," I mouthed to her as we passed. She winked at me as she sipped on her soda.

I let Hailey put me onstage and I sang "I'm a Little Teapot" in front of everyone who was still hanging around. I put up a fight when she filmed it, but just enough to make her feel like I cared. I didn't. I didn't have a tough-guy reputation to uphold. If it made her laugh, I was OK with it. It was the least I could do for her after we'd led her into this party, entirely for our own benefit.

Once I got offstage she said, "Stick around. It'll be time for cake soon."

I checked my watch. Cake was the last step in the party timeline. We were almost at the endgame. Audrey had the right idea coming back to wait. I decided to join her.

"Thanks again for the assist," I said as I slid into the chair across from her.

She shrugged. "I knew you would get out of it, but I thought I could make it easier for you. Oh, by the way, look!" She excitedly pulled out an item from the goodie bag in front of her. "There are tattoos in here! I love these!"

I checked my goodie bag and found a similar sheet of tattoos. I scanned it, ripped off two, and offered the rest of the sheet to her.

"Here. You can have mine."

She gasped. "For real? You don't have to do that."

I shook my head. "Don't sweat it. I'd give you all of them, but I have an idea for these two."

When she smiled at me gratefully, I couldn't help but smile back at her.

She stuck the temporary tattoo sheets into her goodie bag and then looked up at me expectantly. "Well?"

"Well, what?"

"Well, it's my first one of these heist things. How am I doing? And be honest."

"I'm always honest. Ask Conor—I always tell him when he's being an idiot."

"Hey! I'm still on comms, you know."

"Yeah, I know. Case in point."

She laughed. "Oh, I believe you're honest with *him*."

Slight emphasis on the "him." I frowned. "Do you think I lie to you? I know I didn't tell you about what happened at my other school right away but—"

She shook her head and put up a finger before taking her earbuds out and closing her fist around them.

"No. I don't think you're lying to me. Actually, lying isn't the same as just not telling someone something."

"What do you mean?"

"I know . . . you know." When my blank expression just got blanker, she added, "That you kinda like me."

For the first time all night, I had absolutely no idea what to say. My brain suddenly felt like it had licked a

9 volt battery. I froze up completely. "I, uh. How did—"

She pointed at me and tapped her ear twice.

"Oh!" I suddenly remembered I was still on comms and yanked out my earbuds. She couldn't see it, but I felt all the blood in my body rush to my cheeks.

She winced. "Sorry. I wasn't trying to catch you off guard or anything."

"You didn't," I lied, badly. "I just, you know, when did you—*how* did you—?"

She decided to put me out of my misery. "I'm good at reading people. You know that. Also, you were kind of obvious about it." I could tell she was trying to decide whether to keep going or not. After a second, she added, "Also, Conor told me a few days ago."

"What? When?"

"When we were at his house, planning this. You were acting weird. He wanted me to know why you were acting weird so I wouldn't bail on you. Which I wouldn't have done, by the way."

"So you've known this entire time?"

She nodded.

"And?" I did my best to read her, but she was doing the same thing to me. It was like a mirror looking at a mirror. I wasn't getting anything.

Then she smiled a little. "I asked first."

"Huh?"

"I asked a question first and you still haven't answered." I must have still looked confused because she asked again. "How am I doing?"

I couldn't tell if she was teasing me or asking a serious question. Maybe both. I decided to give her a real answer. "Honestly, really good. You're doing things that have names, even though you don't know the names. You just know what to do. I kinda wish this wasn't a one-time thing."

"You want to do another heist?"

"No! I mean . . . kinda?"

She raised an eyebrow at me.

"I dunno, man. There's a reason I used to do this all the time. I really like it.

I was too reckless before, which is why I stopped—but the planning. The close calls. The messing with someone who actually deserves it. Those parts are fun. And working with you too. And, I mean, Conor and Monty. But also you." I felt myself going into idiot-mouth territory, but I couldn't stop myself. Luckily, Audrey chimed in.

"You know we can hang out when this is done, right? I mean, we're in the show together."

"Yeah, but that's only for a couple of weeks."

Now she was looking at me like I was being completely ridiculous. "Yeah, and then we could do other stuff. You know, just hanging out. Normal-style hanging out. Like, maybe we go to the Starcade by school and we actually play games for fun and not to hide from a suspicious manager while we scheme. I actually am pretty good at Skee-Ball."

"You'd wanna do that?"

She shrugged. "Yeah, sure. It sounds like fun. Unless you'd want to do something else?"

"No! I mean, yeah, we should do other stuff too, but

we should for sure do that. You know, when this is over."

"Which should be soon," she said, pointing out a worker just outside the party area who was holding a cake, and coming in our direction.

I nodded and tried to shake off the fuzz in my brain from the conversation. I needed to be sharp. Things were getting down to the wire. "Right. Rain check for the conversation. Game faces now."

I put my earbuds back in.

"Sitting in a tree," Conor was singsonging. "K-I-"

"Conor," I cut in.

"T-T-E-N," he finished quickly. "Kitten. It was stuck in the tree. Hey, DJ. Welcome back to comms."

I rolled my eyes as Audrey put her earbuds back in. "Audrey's back on too, so stop being an idiot. And get back down here. Cake is coming."

"And after cake?" Monty asked, even though he already knew the answer.

"Showtime."

Chapter Nineteen
SHOWTIME

So we sang "Happy Birthday" and ate cake and, you know what? It was good cake. I wasn't so dialed in to the heist that I couldn't appreciate a good ice cream cake. If you ever get so obsessed with something that you don't care about ice cream cake, you've gone too far. That's what I think anyway. I felt a little bad that Monty basically had to listen to us eat over comms. Conor offered to smuggle him out a slice but he said it was OK.

"Plus," he said, "I got a cookie when I was outside before."

Cake was the last structured event of the party. After that, we were basically just supposed to hang around until we got picked up.

As the party wound down, I licked ice cream off the back of my fork and looked over the party area. About half the invited kids were still around. The rest had either filtered back onto the game floor or been picked up by their parents. Conor had already dipped out, and other kids were starting to leave too. One of them was Tyler.

"Hey, man," he said, sidling over to my table. "My mom just texted me. I'm about to head out. But before I do, your friend told me to hold something for you?" He held up a giant black garbage bag of tickets. "I thought you were gonna come get it, but you never did and I didn't see you all party." Clearly, he hadn't been around for my award-winning rendition of "I'm a Little Teapot." "Do you want it now?"

I took the bag. "Thanks, man. See you in class tomorrow."

"Yeah, man. See ya." We fist-bumped and he started moving off. Before he did, I stopped him. I couldn't help it.

"Hey, Tyler?"

"Sup?"

"Did you notice anything weird about Hailey today?"

"Duh," he said. "How could I not? I mean, man. That girl is *really* into karaoke. What's that about, right?"

Right. Karaoke. "Just making sure it wasn't just me." I waved as he left for real and then said over comms, "I got the package." I didn't get a reply. I didn't expect one. Everyone else was busy.

I scanned the room. Hailey was standing at the entrance to the party area, saying bye to people as they left. I gave her a couple of minutes to give what I was sure would be an extended goodbye to Tyler before coming over myself.

"Heading out, Flounder?" she said.

"Yeah, I think my mom is coming to pick me up soon. Really great party though. Thanks for inviting me."

"Thanks for coming," she said, grabbing me in a hug. When she was close enough, she also added in a whisper, "And I think the whole thing with Tyler went pretty well too. He was def picking up my signals."

"Mm-hm," I said noncommittally. Like I said, there's a reason I never did romance jobs.

When I pulled back, Hailey noticed the bag of tickets I was holding. "Dang. Did you get all of those tonight?"

"Yeah. I guess I had kind of a hot streak."

She whistled. "You gotta teach me your tricks. Ooh! Starcade after-party once we wrap the show? What do you think? You can show me how you won all those tickets."

"Sounds really fun." It also gave me an idea, but I put a pin in it for later. "Well, see ya, Ariel."

"Bye, Flounder."

I grabbed my bag of tickets and checked that the coast was clear before exiting the party area. I had a straight shot to the door. As I walked between the arcade cabinets, lights blinking on and off around me, I felt my heartbeat start to go into overdrive. We were so close. So close to getting out with the tickets.

The only thing between me and the door was—suddenly standing between me and the door. And he looked smug. I tried to turn back, but he wasn't having that.

"No, no, no," he said, putting up a hand. "Don't turn around. You really thought I wasn't going to find the tickets, huh? But why would I waste time searching this whole arcade when I knew you had to take them out eventually? You're not leaving here with stolen tickets."

I couldn't duck this. His face was set, determined. And he was talking loud enough for other people to hear. Like, he didn't just want to be right, he wanted other people to know it. At his accusation, a couple of people turned around to look at me.

"Well?" he said.

"Well what? I didn't steal the tickets."

"We'll see about that," he said. "Open the bag."

"But—"

"Open the bag," he said.

"You're not a cop."

"But I am the manager. Open the bag or I will have you banned for life."

"Fine." I hesitantly pulled the bag forward, untied the top, and there they were. Strings and strings of Starcade tickets. All of them with the ridges from being dispensed from an arcade cabinet. Not smooth tickets straight from a roll. "See? Not stolen. Can I go now?"

He seemed thrown for a second, but then his face changed. "Oh! The trash! You weren't going for the ticket rolls in the back. You were going for the alley. The tickets are literally in a trash bag!"

"Excuse me," a familiar voice said. I turned. It was Hailey's mom. Apparently, the commotion had been even louder than I'd thought. "What is going on here?"

"Sorry, ma'am," Tony said. "Arcade business."

"This is one of my daughter's friends," she said, stepping closer to me. "Why are you yelling at him?"

I don't think Tony liked being outside of a customer's good graces, but he stood his ground. "This little delinquent stole tickets from the trash. Show her."

"I didn't steal any tickets," I repeated. "Smell them. If they were from the trash, wouldn't they smell like trash?"

Mrs. Coombs sniffed the tickets. "They don't smell like

trash." She put her hands on her hips and looked at Tony expectantly.

He took a quick sniff of the bag, looked disappointed, and then quickly recovered. "I don't know what you did about the smell, but there's no way you won all those tickets in the past two hours. I've been watching you."

"You've been watching him?" Mrs. Coombs said.

"No, not like that. He's just been acting suspicious and—"

"What about him is suspicious?" Now even more people were watching. The way Mrs. Coombs was talking, this clearly wasn't her first rodeo. She was about as dramatic as Hailey, and she wasn't even onstage.

"Ma'am, all I'm saying is that this boy has been doing a lot of sneaking around tonight and not a lot of game playing and I don't think that there's any way he—"

"I'll prove it," I said, fishing a token out of my pocket and starting toward the other side of the arcade.

"What are you—"

"I'll show you where the tickets came from." I marched all the way over to Rowdy Roundup, a small crowd of spectators behind me. "Restart the machine," I said.

"Huh?"

"Restart the machine. So you know I didn't cheat."

Realization started to spread across Tony's face, but he was trapped. He reluctantly put his manager's code into the machine and it rebooted. Once it was back online, I slotted in a token and started playing.

Farm animals began to fall from the top of the screen. Cows, sheep, pigs. I matched them, but not too quickly. I copied Laura and the guy from the other Starcade. Matches, but not too many matches. Clear the board, but not too fast. Get the stacks close to the foul line, but never above it. Clear the animals, but clear them in big batches. There was a pattern to it. Place the animals correctly and they'd clear so that the ones that fell would land and clear another row and on and on until the board was empty. I was con-centrating too much on the screen to see my score, but I could hear the plink-plink-plink as the number went up higher and higher with every cascade of animals cleared.

With a final pig in place, the board cleared and a jackpot symbol flashed on-screen. Ticket after ticket poured from the machine. I let them scroll out without taking them. Then, I turned back to Tony. "Do you believe me now?"

Expressions flashed across his face—shock, annoyance, confusion.

"But—wait—"

"But nothing," Mrs. Coombs said. "Who's your boss? I want to talk to your boss." A perfect Aunt Karen, except she was dead serious.

"Ma'am, I—"

While she gave him the third degree, I took my bag and walked right over to Duke, who, of course, had been filming the whole thing. When I came over, he lowered the camera, as if the jig wasn't already up.

"You saw all that?" I asked.

"How could I not?" he said. "She's so loud, I think everyone in the whole Starcade heard her." He was right.

I even saw some red shirts sniggering at Tony on the down low around the floor.

"Well, that's lucky. Very *lucky*."

"Huh?"

"Give these to your boss with the footage." I handed him the two temporary tattoos I'd kept.

"What?"

Before he could work out what I meant, I shoved the bag of tickets in his hands. "And here. You can keep the change."

He blinked at me, confused. "But . . . wait. But I thought that . . . Don't you need—?"

"Don't worry about it," I said walking toward the door. "Just enjoy. And go home. That's what I'm going to do."

And I did.

But not before I checked on one last thing.

Chapter Twenty
THE MOONWALKING BEAR

There's this video on YouTube. There are a bunch of guys outside. Half of them are in black shirts, half of them are in white shirts, and each team has a basketball. The announcer asks you to keep track of how many passes the team in white makes, so you concentrate on them as both teams are weaving and dipping in and around each other and you probably come up with the right answer.

But then, the announcer asks, "But did you see the moonwalking bear?"

And you have no idea what he's talking about so you rewind the video and you ignore all the jumping around and passing the teams are doing, and right there, smack in the middle of everything, is a guy in a black bear costume, moonwalking across the screen. The moonwalking bear. Right under your nose the whole time, but you didn't notice because you were paying attention to something else.

Say, for instance, some very purposefully clumsy attempts to break into the employee-only area of a certain Starcade. Some very obvious shows of exaggerated sneakiness. And a great big, suspicious garbage bag of tickets going out the front door while the rest of my team were perfecting their moonwalks.

While I had been tuning out the rest of my team, they'd been tuning me out too. Like I said before, they were busy. Busier than me really. I was only the distraction, after all.

I'd paid attention, just enough to hear that things had kicked off properly. That Monty had gone back to the bakery right next to the Starcade, the one he'd stepped into while we were eating pizza with the rest of the party guests.

"Excuse me," Monty had said, repeating after Audrey. "Did you take out the trash? I think I accidentally dropped something in there when I was in here earlier."

It was a rhetorical question, of course. We knew they'd taken out the trash. We were counting on it. That's why Monty had dropped a napkin soaked in Conor's fart spray into the trash the first time he was in there.

That was enough to get Monty in the alley, with the dumpsters the Starcade and the bakery shared. But it wasn't enough to stop the bakery owner from questioning why he was grabbing trash bags out of the trash and taking them out. Which is why Audrey was in the bakery, distracting him.

"I'm just not sure about what to put on the cake," I heard her saying over comms as I walked away from Duke. "She really likes cats, but I don't know if she'd want one on a cake, you know? Because then she'd have to cut into it and that would be weird. What do you think?"

Perfect, as usual. Which meant Monty was on the inside of the fence, snatching bags of tickets out of the dumpster and tossing them over. I didn't want to break his concentration either. So I talked to Conor.

"How are you guys doing, Con?"

271

"I think we have enough," he said. He was on the other side of the fence, catching the bags Monty threw over.

"And Felix is——?"

"Already here," Conor said. "We're loading the bags into his truck right now."

"Great." Laura had given me the idea. She hated Tony enough to help us out. She'd even let me have her giant trash bag of tickets—the one I'd just used as a decoy—on the condition that I sent her the video of us embarrassing Tony in front of everyone. Maybe Felix would be willing to break his promise to never come back to the Starcade if it was to pull one over on the reason he'd made that promise.

I had Monty make the call, and according to him, it had taken less than no convincing. Felix had started driving over before he even got off the phone.

"Tell him he'll have his video once I get it from Duke." Originally, I was going to have Conor be my videographer, but with Duke roped in, I decided to put him outside so Monty would have more help. Tony causing a scene created the distraction Conor needed to walk out the front door without alerting the employee at the door and, party over, Audrey had snipped off her birthday band and slipped out herself.

"Guys, he's coming to check on Monty!" Audrey hissed from inside the bakery. "You have, like, twenty seconds! Go!"

I heard a rustle and then the slamming of a truck door. "We'll loop around and get you, Monty," said Conor. "Hang tight."

From the door of the Starcade, I saw the truck peel away from the front of the bakery and drive to the other side of the shopping plaza. Out of sight, out of danger.

Over comms, Audrey was coaching Monty through pretending that he'd found his emergency credit card, which he'd never lost in the first place. She was on top of it.

I turned back to the game floor. Mrs. Coombs was still giving Tony the verbal smackdown of his life. I would have felt bad—he was kinda right after all—except for the way he treated Monty. I'd said I wasn't going to hurt any innocent bystanders, but, as far as I was concerned, picking on a kid less than half your age disqualified you from that classification.

I didn't feel like I had after my last job. Honestly, I didn't feel like I usually did after my other jobs either. It felt better. I wasn't working with a mercenary team, put together just for the job. I was working with people I liked. Even Monty was really growing on me. I wasn't doing it for a payout. I was doing it to save Conor. Save him from a mess he made, sure, but it still felt good.

And now it was over.

One last job to save Conor. That was always the plan. I was still out.

I felt my phone buzz and checked. It was my mom. She was in the parking lot, about to pick me up.

"OK, guys," I said. "My mom is here. I'm signing off comms, but call me if you need me. Good job out there today. You all really, really killed it."

"Dude, switching to a Moonwalking Bear midway through like that? Like, I know we talked about it before as, like, a Plan Z, but I didn't think you'd be crazy enough to run it with two newbies on their first job."

"I knew they could handle it," I said. Audrey's seamless Crybaby play at the Starcade dumpster on her first day on the team and Monty's fifteen-minute flip from scary stranger to all-in ally had made me sure they were adaptable enough to roll with the punches of a last-minute Moonwalking Bear swap. "They were the MVPs for sure."

"Well, we wouldn't have been able to do any of this without you and Conor," Audrey said. "So we should just split the credit and—you know what? I'm going to have to think about it some more. But maybe I can just buy a cookie for now?" She slipped perfectly back into Face mode like a curtain had lifted onstage. Even just her voice change over the phone was wild.

"We'll start laundering the tickets tomorrow," I said. "Talk to you guys later." And then I switched off comms.

When I got home, I didn't go right to bed. I'd done my homework beforehand—it was a condition of getting to go to the party—but there was a little extracurricular research I wanted to do first.

The next day, we tied up loose ends. True to his word, Duke sent me the videos he'd taken. I watched the footage of him stalking us to see if there was anything too incriminating. Satisfied that there wasn't, I deleted everything except the video of me and Tony, which I sent to both Laura and Felix, who were very appreciative.

After school, the whole gang of us helped with the laundering. We'd been planning on spreading it out over the week but the new ticket-counter machines were lightning fast. With the four of us working together, we were done that same day. Even though we'd promised Audrey all the leftover tickets, she insisted on an even split. When we counted up our take, it added up to a little less than double what we needed to bail Conor out.

We made him buy the round of celebration candy from the prize counter after that.

We'd put the receipts through the machines two thousand tickets at a time, so I divided up the leftovers between us and stowed Lucky's cut in my pockets. It was a lot to keep on me, but I also felt like it was too much to not keep on me. What if my mom thought the receipts were junk and threw them away or something? It probably wouldn't happen, but I didn't need that stress in my life, so I just stuck them in there and slept in my jeans.

Conor was at school before me the next day for the first time ever. He caught me coming off the bus and he was jumping around like he was walking on hot pavement barefoot.

"Did you bring them?" he asked.

"No. After all that, I left them at home on the day they matter." I rolled my eyes. "What do you think, Conor?"

"Sorry, I'm just nervous. I know we got the tickets and everything, but dealing with this much currency at once is always iffy. You know that."

I did. This wasn't my first rodeo. "Don't worry," I said. "Lucky doesn't scare me."

"Lucky not scaring me is what got us in this mess."

"Yeah, but that means I have you as an example of

what not to do. As usual." I cuffed him on the shoulder playfully. Then, after a second, I hit him again, harder this time.

"Ow! What was that for?"

"For telling Audrey I like her!"

"Well, excuse me for trying to help a guy out!" He suddenly stopped rubbing his shoulder and perked up. "Wait, if you know I told her, then that means she told you! What did she say?"

"None of your business, Conor."

"Oh, come on. Just tell me."

He kept bugging me until class started but my lips were sealed.

The night before, I'd worked out how I was going to slip out of my math class to go see Lucky, but it ended up being a waste of effort. First period, I got a massive wave of déjà vu and a summons to the front office. The message was the same as the first time. *Library. Third period. Don't be late.* And a butterfly for Mariposa.

That's the thing about when you owe people. You

don't have to worry about finding them. They find you.

Lucky sat at his usual table, and this time, Mariposa wasn't at the door near the comics. She was sitting at his right hand. Under her left shirtsleeve, I could just see the bright purple of a butterfly temporary tattoo. Lucky wasn't wearing the matching shamrock I'd given to Duke, at least not in a place I could see, but that was OK. It was mostly for Mariposa's benefit.

"DJ," Lucky said, gesturing to the seat across from him. "Glad you could make it."

"Did I really have a choice?"

"You always have a choice," he replied, but the little smirk on his lips told me that he didn't believe what he was saying. Not really. Still, I took the seat as casually as I dared to without tipping my hand.

"So," he said, just as casually. "How are you doing, DJ? How is life treating you?"

I snorted. "Great. I love getting ominously summoned in the middle of the school day. We should do this more often."

"Oh, come on, DJ. Can't we chat? I'm an interesting guy. You're an interesting guy."

I crossed my arms. "You wanna chat? Fine. What did you think of the party?"

"What party?" he said innocently.

"Hailey's party."

He gave an airy shrug. "I wouldn't know. I wasn't at the party. I didn't get where I am by going to every kid's birthday party. I don't even know which Hailey you're talking about."

I glanced over at Mariposa and her tattoo and then back at him. "Sure. Now, do you wanna get down to business or what?" I knew he must have known or at least guessed that I had the tickets based on Duke's report, or else why would he have called me in before my time was up?

He spread his hands out in front of me. "By all means. Show me what you got."

I reached into my pocket and pulled out a stack of Starcade receipts. "One hundred thousand tickets and some change, just like I promised. You want me to add it up for you?"

He thumbed through the stack quickly and then pushed it to the side. "No need. I can tell it's enough without doing any math."

"So I'm free to go, then." I started to get up, but Mariposa blocked my path before I could take even one step forward. "Or not."

"Relax," Lucky said, gesturing to my seat. "We're chatting, remember?"

"Right." I sat back down. "So, Lucky. What do you want to chat about? The weather? The baseball game next week?"

"Mmm, I was thinking more along the lines of how you got all these tickets in less than two weeks."

Now it was my turn to play dumb. "Where does anyone get tickets? From a Starcade. You should know. You have more tickets than anyone." I pointed at the stack I'd slid to him. "Even more now."

"You're right," he said. "I do know what it takes to

make this many tickets in so little time. Which is why I'm so curious about how you managed to pull it off."

He paused for me to answer, and when I didn't, he frowned. "Well?"

"Well what?"

"You know what." I did, but I wanted him to say it. "You and I both know that what I asked you to do was impossible through normal means, and yet somehow, you did it."

I shrugged. "Like you said, I'm an interesting guy."

"Very," he agreed. "And, as I'm sure you know, I like to surround myself with interesting people." He picked up a folder from the chair next to him and slid it over to me.

I looked at it and then at him without picking it up. He nodded his head toward it. "Open it. I got it printed special."

I opened the folder and scanned the first few lines: *Permanent position. 1,000 tickets per week retainer. Protection detail.*

"Are you offering me a job? Working for you?"

"What can I say? I like hiring the best, and clearly, you're the best. You'll get a weekly stipend of tickets, unlimited hall passes—oh, and, Mariposa, make sure he gets a reserved spot anywhere in the cafeteria during his lunch period. You still have your hookup, right?"

"Of course."

"Perfect." He gave me a big, toothy grin. "And that's just for starters. Everything is outlined in that contract, which I'm sure you'll want to read, but then we can just shake hands and—"

"No."

"No? Oh, don't worry. We'd both sign it too, of course. Gotta be official. And then—"

"I mean no, I'm not going to work for you."

"With me."

"That either. I did this to bail out Conor. That's it. I'm not going to be your errand boy or your mercenary or whatever it is you want me to be." I closed the folder. "That's not who I am."

"Isn't it though? Because, well, that's what Conor told

me. And you did get the tickets. So, what am I supposed to think here, DJ? Help me out?"

"You're not supposed to think anything," I said, keeping my voice quiet and level but as firm as possible. "You're supposed to take what I owe you and let me go. Or do I not have a choice here?"

We stared each other down for a few beats. Then he pulled out a Twizzler and chomped down on it. "You're right. You do have a choice. Of course, some choices are smarter than others. I'm sure a smart guy like you knows that. And I don't know how smart it would be for you to turn down this job offer, considering that, if you're not working for me, I might be forced to see you as a threat. And I don't think either of us would want that, would we?"

"No. Which is why it's a good thing that I already told you that that's not who I am."

"That's what you say, but how can I be sure? I mean, I don't want to use the nuclear option, of course."

"Of course."

"But if you force my hand . . ." He trailed off ominously.

There was another couple of beats of silence, but, this time, I broke it.

"AP."

He frowned—an actual, genuine frown of confusion and surprise, not a rehearsed Big Boss mask. "What?"

"AP," I said again. "Do you know what it stands for?" When he didn't answer, I said, "Someone said it to me the other day at the Starcade, and I didn't know what it meant so I looked it up. It stands for Advantage Player. You know, like a guy who counts cards at casinos? That's where it comes from, but arcade players use it too. The really high-level ones who rack up tickets for big prizes and then flip them for profit online. You know, like your cousin who left you all the tickets he made from Skee-Ball."

The explanation seemed to make him more confused. "So? That was just startup capital. Now that I'm established, it doesn't matter."

"Not to you," I agreed. "And Skee-Ball is about aim and throwing power. Understanding how the game works isn't gonna give you an arm like Tyler or your cousin. But what if someone, let's say me, met some APs recently. Hypothetically, of course. And what if I watched them play a game that actually doesn't take that much skill at all. A game that just takes memorizing a pattern that's pretty simple once you know what you're looking for. What if the method was so reliable that you could hit the jackpot pretty much every game in a row?" As I said those last couple of words, I placed down three Starcade receipts from three different rows of tickets. Each exactly one thousand tickets. "And what if it wasn't just that one game? Hypothetically?"

He inspected the receipts and then frowned. "Hypothetically, I don't see how that would help your case."

"It wouldn't if I just wanted to use it to rack up tickets and challenge you. I'm guessing it would be a good way for me to get rocket boosted. But here's the thing, Lucky. I wouldn't use it for that. I wouldn't use it at all. I'd give it away."

His eyes widened. "What?"

"I'd give it away," I repeated. "To everyone. Everyone in the entire school."

I could see him trying to connect dots in his head. "But . . . how would that help you?"

"It wouldn't. That's not the point. Do you know what happens when too much currency enters the economy at the same time? Inflation. It becomes worthless. If anyone with a couple of tokens can net an easy jackpot in a couple of minutes, then how impressive are you? Less, I bet." As realization began to dawn on him, I kept talking. "And, not that I pay too much attention to school politics, but tickets are basically your whole thing, right? You're not like a Tyler or a Hailey. You just bought the school. Before you had tickets, you really didn't have anything, did you?"

His face tightened a little bit, like I'd hit a nerve. Then he said, "It wouldn't last long. I know how the machines work. If any of the games start paying out too many tickets, they adjust them so the jackpot is lower, or they make the machine pay out less often."

"True," I said. That's basically what Conor had reported

back to me after looking over the operating manual for the Whirlwind. Rigged, just like I'd thought. Even if someone had lightning-fast reflexes, the machine wouldn't pay out more than it was set to.

"They'll change it, but not right away. And based on the attention span middle schoolers have, I'm guessing it will take more time for the manager to change the machine than it'll take the school to turn to a new currency like holos or rubber bracelets or popularity. Hypothetically speaking, of course."

"Of course."

Another staredown, and this time, I dropped my poker face and let him really see how un-hypothetical everything I'd said was. He stared back, eyes just as hard, lips stained red, nostrils flaring like he was a bull, and . . .

And he laughed. He relaxed back in his seat and he laughed.

"Well played, DJ. What did I say, Mariposa? I told you this guy was sharp." He nodded at her and she stepped out of my way. "Get out of here."

I got up, slowly. "Are we done?"

"We're . . . at an impasse. You painted me into a corner. I respect that. But I never stay in a corner for very long. I mean, you know where I started. And look where I am. If I were you, DJ, I'd watch my back."

I pushed the chair back and left the receipts on the table. "That's funny. I was going to say the same thing to you."

And I left the library.

Everyone wanted a debrief on how the meeting went right away, but after a job, lying low is almost always the best option. We'd been discreet enough that I didn't think anyone at the party knew we were working together, but with Duke's footage, Lucky definitely did. I could feel a tail on me all day, and I was sure the others were being followed too. I didn't see anyone in the group again until twenty minutes after school ended, at Audrey's place.

I was the last one there. I only got through a knock and a half before Conor opened the door, grabbed my wrist, and dragged me through.

"Finally!" he said, barely giving me enough time to shut the door behind me. "We've been waiting forever."

I rolled my eyes at his impatience, but let myself get dragged through the foyer and into the living room, where Monty and Audrey were already waiting.

"So?" Audrey said when she saw me. "Are we having celebration ice cream cones or last meal ice cream cones?"

"What's the difference?"

She grinned. "Second one has more chocolate sauce."

I couldn't help but grin back. "Well, I hope you don't like chocolate sauce, because—"

Before I even finished, Conor tackled me to the ground roughly.

"Yes!" he crowed. "I knew it! I knew you'd come through!"

"Can't . . . breathe," I just managed to choke out. Monty got up from the couch and pulled Conor off me. "Phew. Thanks, man."

"Sorry. Got a little excited. But we're all good?"

I nodded. "He took the payment. And he didn't call my bluff."

I hadn't actually cracked any of the games besides Rowdy Roundup. Most of the serious AP tricks were hidden on password-protected, invitation-only message boards. Realistically, one game wasn't enough to ruin the ticket economy, but the threat of a ruined economy was enough to stop Lucky, at least for now.

"You're not getting rocket boosted. We're not getting rocket boosted. I'm not getting forcibly recruited into Lucky's operation. I mean, not until he figures a way out of my fail-safe, but I don't think he will anytime soon. We are all good."

Conor fist-pumped. Then he stopped. "What do we do now?"

"What do you mean?"

He gave me a *come on* kind of look. "You know what I mean." He gestured to the four of us. "What's next? For us."

"Ice cream, I think," I said.

"Oh, come on!" he moaned. "Don't lie to yourself.

You're telling me this doesn't make you wanna get back in the game?"

"What part of *retired* do you not understand?"

"It's a waste of talent! It's like keeping four Porsches in the garage! Tell him, Monty!"

"Will we still hang out, even though we're not heisting?" Monty asked.

"Sure."

Monty smiled and Conor made a face. "No! DJ! Gah. Audrey, help me out here."

But before he was done talking, Audrey caught my eye and started dragging me away, to the kitchen. And, unlike Conor, who had grabbed me by the wrist, she grabbed me by the hand. He kept calling after me, but I ignored him. I mean, looking for trouble or eating ice cream with Audrey?

You didn't have to be the Brains of the operation to make that choice.

Epilogue
CURTAIN CALL

The energy backstage was electric.

Everyone was loud and everyone was bumping into each other and absolutely no one cared.

"Oh my gosh," I heard Hailey say from the other side of the room. "I think that was even better than last night. Even with the little mistake with my tail. I played it off, right?"

While everyone let her know that she totally had, I scanned the mosh pit of kids for Audrey. I frowned. That was weird. She was usually pretty easy to spot. So why couldn't I—

Cold hands suddenly covered my eyes from behind.

"Audrey! Did you have your hands in a freezer or something?"

"Ah, come on," she said, not sounding very disappointed. "You could at least act surprised one time." When she moved to face me, she was grinning. "So, that was our last show. What did you think?"

"It was fun," I said. "Not really my thing, but I see why you like it. And it was fun to do it with you."

She smiled bashfully, before launching back into excited chatting. "Hey! I heard a rumor that we're doing *Into the Woods Jr.* next year. Mark my words, I am going to play a witch before we graduate."

"I have complete faith in you."

It seemed like she was about to start talking again, but, before she could, one of the teachers poked her head through the curtains and caught my attention. "Oh, there you are, DJ. Someone wants to talk to you. Do you have a minute?"

Audrey looked at me questioningly, and I shrugged. My parents had already come to see me in the first show. Monty and Conor were at that show too. I didn't know who else would want to visit me backstage.

"Sure, send them in." When I saw who it was, I grew even more confused. "David? What are you doing here?" I mean, don't get me wrong. I liked the guy fine, but we had more of a professional relationship. That and he looked kind of nervous.

"Hey, DJ. Can we talk?" He glanced at the crowd. "Somewhere else?"

"What about the prop closet?" Audrey suggested, leading us over there before I had a chance to agree. "I'll make sure no one bothers you." She ushered us into the room and I flicked the light on right as she closed the door.

"What's going on?" I asked. "Why did you have to talk to me in such a hurry?"

"I'm sorry, but it's important. And I couldn't do it during school hours. Too many ears." Now I was even more curious. "I have this client," he continued. "She's having some problems."

I put up my hands to stop him. "Whoa, whoa, whoa. What about client confidentiality and all that?"

"I have permission to be talking to you. And, I wouldn't have even asked for it except . . ."

"Except?"

"You're the only person I know who's done it. Who's been targeted by Lucky and somehow escaped."

I tensed. "Lucky? David, I told you. I don't do that anymore. I'm clean. *You* said I should get a hobby. I got one!"

"I know. And you don't have to say yes. But this kid . . . it's a bad situation and it's not her fault. Some of Lucky's goods got misplaced. It was a wrong place, wrong time thing. She's the main target and she swears she's being set up. But if she can't prove it . . ."

"One-way ticket to Pluto," I finished.

"I know her. I know she's telling the truth. And I know I said your whole thing was unhealthy, but . . . maybe this is different. Helping people. Not just doing it for the thrill."

I hesitated. Conor had been right weeks ago. I did still love what I did. It was like nothing else. I'd only been suppressing it because I'd thought it was the right thing to do.

But what if David was right too? What if I could do what I'd been doing, but not for whoever would pay me. For people who needed it? People who deserved it. It could be a whole new era. The same, but different. Using my talents without the guilt in the pit of my stomach.

"So, what do you say?" David asked, snapping me out of my thoughts.

"I—" I started, but then I realized, it wasn't just my decision.

"I have to talk to my crew," I said instead. And, luckily, one member of my crew was just outside, keeping watch.

I cracked the door open. "Audrey I . . . *we* might have another job."

And, before I could explain it or ask her opinion or say anything other than that one sentence, she got that look in her eye. That hawk look. She grinned.

"You call Conor. I'll call Monty. I'm in."

ACKNOWLEDGMENTS

After years of flipping past these in books, it's finally time for me to write one! To plan a heist, you need a great team, and it's the same for getting a book published.

A huge shout-out to my rock-star agent, Emily, who saw the potential in this idea from our very first phone call and my awesome editor, Anna, along with the whole Scholastic team, who helped me make it the best version of itself.

I'd like to thank Sharon, Melanie, and Camille for beta reading the original manuscript and helping me get it in tip-top shape.

I, of course, have to thank my mom and dad for encouraging my writing and keeping me supplied with books to keep my nose in while growing up.

And finally, I'd like to thank my brother, Michael, who is as clever as DJ, as tough as Monty, as charming as Audrey, and as trouble-prone as Conor, for having such a shenanigans-filled middle school career that this book was practically an inevitability.